WYOMING DREAMER

C J CLARK

Cover Photo: The Clouds Have Fallen by Jack Sanders, Mesa, AZ.

ACKNOWLEDGMENTS

Many thanks go to D'Ann Linscott Dunham for her invaluable horse and ranching expertise; to Terri Guy and Nirvana Farhadi for their help in editing; and to Jennie Lewis who can always bring me out of writer's block.

CHAPTER ONE

"No! No!" Page Chandling cried. She bit her lip. Tensed. Awaited her fate. She clenched the steering wheel. Took her foot off the gas. Prayed under her breath as the Taurus fishtailed from lane to lane over the snow covered icy mountain road. She turned the wheel this way and that as she tried to correct its path. The car slid closer . . . closer . . . to the edge. *God help me*, she prayed. She closed her eyes, heard the swooshing snow, waited for the impact, the pain, but it did not come. The Taurus skidded a little farther until it came to a sudden stop.

Cracking one eye open at a time, she assessed where she was—perched precariously on the edge of the roadbed thousands of feet above a steep valley. She sat a moment catching her breath, calming her nerves before pulling on the door latch. It wouldn't budge. Maybe she could get out on the passenger side. But if she inched over, would it send the car plummeting? She had to try. She minced her way across the seat. Rubbing the steam off the window, she gasped seeing the depth of the valley below. Looking down and around, the compacted snow was all that had kept her from sliding into oblivion, tumbling repeatedly through a mass of snow-encrusted cedars, pines and unforgiving rock. Instant death. Or an agonizingly slow one if she lay hidden at the bottom, a mass of broken bones.

She tried opening the passenger door. It too would not budge. Peering through a small clear space in the windshield, out in the distance, the Black Hills lay covered in coruscated snow. How could anything so beautiful turn so deadly? The marble sized flakes at the lower elevations had turned into blizzard-like conditions here at seven thousand feet. She bumped up the dual defrost-heat slide. Why wouldn't the doors open? Was it that cold outside? The windshield wipers thwacked out their rhythmic dance as the defroster thrummed, working overtime, trying to keep the ice from building up on the windshield. Nevertheless, even the higher temperature could not defrost the slushy ice fast enough.

She shivered. Her cotton slacks and long sleeved jersey shirt were too thin for the inclement weather. However, it had not been snowing when she left the motel nestled in the foothills of Newcastle, Wyoming. The sun had been out; she had been adequately dressed. How could she have known she would run into a blizzard? Here, the skies were gray, the wind boisterous, and visibility nearly nil.

She flicked the defroster all the way to max. Within seconds, the windows steamed over to where she couldn't see out. Ice formations crystallized on the windshield and windows. A blast of wind shook the car making her grab the seat, afraid it might blow the car over the edge. Too scared to try rocking the vehicle for fear it would spin the tires and shimmy the car over the precipice, she tried the door again to no avail. She butted the driver's door with her shoulder, tried rolling down the windows. Frozen tight.

Stupid, stupid, stupid. You and your stupid mountain man-survivalist wannabe ideas. Well Page, this is a fine mess you've gotten yourself into. You just had to go exploring; you just had to go up into the mountains.

Steady shivering overtook her as the dampness crept into the car. Goose bumps prickled her skin. Her teeth chattered. As the windows glazed over, she remembered that snow was an insulator. She could never understand that. Snow was cold. It might insulate a soda can keeping it cold, but how did snow keep anything warm? Still, it was a theory the experts touted and she assumed they knew their business and at least she shouldn't freeze, but the cold permeated her by the minute. She rubbed her arms and thighs, then switched the defroster to maximum heat. The heat and the running engine should melt the ice bound Taurus. She hoped. If so, she could get out and walk for help. Meanwhile, she turned the radio on scanning the frequencies. Only one static filled station came through.

". . . whiteout . . . crackle . . . crackle . . . treacherous roads. . . Do not attempt driving . . . crackle . . ." Static took over. She turned the radio off.

"Great, just great. I haven't seen a car for at least ten miles. I'm all alone and no one to find me." Hoping against hope she was wrong, she resolved to wait for help. Surely, someone lived on this road. Someone had to come along eventually. She put the hazard lights on, shut off the ice-encrusted wipers and nestled into the seat. Squinting, she tried to see through the windshield. The visibility was almost zero.

Within minutes, opaque layers of ice glazed the windows. Her breath quickened. Would anyone see the car? Was it ice covered? What if they didn't see her, hit her, sent her over the edge? *Please God, send somebody to find me.* She turned the headlights on hoping it would make the vehicle more visible.

Only a week in Wyoming and look at the predicament I'm in. Stay calm. . . Stay calm. She thought about Sammy, her yellow tabby, back in the motel in Newcastle. *Why did I ever leave you? What if I never see you again? Some survivalist I am.*

She yawned, finding it hard to stay awake. The warm air blasting from the defroster/heater lulled her into a sleepy state. As her eyelids drooped, she jerked fighting to keep them open. Sleepy, so sleepy. Her eyes closed. She swallowed hard. Parched. Her throat felt scratchy. She groaned rubbing the area between her eyebrows. *Must be getting a sinus headache. If I could just get some fresh air. .*

Grabbing the door handle again, she tried valiantly to open it. When it didn't budge, she rubbed the clouded windshield only to view a solid sheet of ice. *Entombed!* Her heart beat erratically faster and faster until she thought she was going into cardiac arrest. A wave of nausea rolled over her. *Uhhhhhh, I think I'm going to be sick.* Shivering, she felt an urge to go to the bathroom if she didn't throw up first. Her eyes darted over the contents in the car. No fast food cups, no bottles. Too late, she found a box of Kleenex. Her wet pants instantly felt like ice cubes against her skin just before she passed out.

* * * *

Quaid Kincaid scratched his head, looked out at the drifting snow and took a last swig of lukewarm black coffee before heading out the door. A blast of artic air greeted him pricking his nostrils like needles and making his eyes water. He tipped his Stetson a little lower to shade the bright snow glare, shoved his arms into a sheep lined jacket, and then pulled up the collar. He blew on his hands before inserting them into heavy gloves. "Sure as hell's cold this morning. Can't remember ever havin' a snowstorm this early in the year." He was glad he had put his long johns and extra wool socks on this morning.

Wading through snowdrifts, snow fell down into the tops of his boots as the cold air seeped through his Carhartt bibs.

After opening the barn doors, he hoisted himself into the cab of the tractor and turned the key in the ignition. The motor started right up. Pulling a lever, the attached snowblade raised. Shifting the heavy monster into gear, it lurched forward crunching the pristine snow under its huge tires.

At the edge of the drive he stopped to look out at the blowing, drifting snow building up on the county road. Some spots were almost bare where the wind had swept the road clean while other areas had to be six foot deep. The high altitude winds, combined with the sleet, left a crusty layer of ice over the snow making it slippery, but he felt confident the weight of the tractor would keep him on course.

He was thankful his parents had left him the tractor-snowplow before passing the ranch on to him. It made his job a little easier and helped fulfill his responsibility to the community. Lack of county road workers meant the locals had to pitch in or face being snowbound and Quaid always wanted to do his share.

He stopped as he neared Kyle Fisher's fence line. "What the—" A barely visible, ice-encrusted vehicle sat on the edge of the road. A patch of paint peeked from a warm spot on the hood. Was the car running? Was someone inside?

Quaid shifted the tractor to idle. He jumped out then ran to the vehicle. It was running. Knocking on the glass, he peered through the glazed windows. Unable to see anything, he walked around the vehicle spotting the snow packed tailpipe. Springing into action, he kicked and dug as much snow away from the tailpipe as he could before running back to the door. Thumping his fist on it, the ice cracked but did not break.

"Anyone in there? You all right?" he shouted. His warm breath on the window left a wet spot. He pounded on the iced door latch trying to open it. But it was to no avail A sickening dread spread through him. He ran to the tractor and found a crowbar. Prying at the car door, miniscule chips of ice broke away. Making a dash for the back window, he swung the crowbar with all his might. Shattering into millions of fragments, it left a gaping hole of easy access to crawl through. Once inside, he saw her.

"Shit! Carbon monoxide. Dumb broad," he muttered. His eyes teared and he began coughing.

A young woman with blonde hair lay slumped in the seat passed out at the wheel. Her pale skin, cyanotic lips and fingernails testified to lack of oxygen.

He crawled over the seat, shut the ignition and the headlights off, and then quickly looked her over for injuries. Overcome by the noxious gas, he fell back in the rear seat, coughing from the fumes. Pulling himself up through the rear windshield, he stuck his head outside, gulping in freshets of air before returning to her. Looking around for a coat or blanket to wrap around her he found neither. Alarmed she wasn't responding to the blast of fresh air, he cupped his hands around her neck, rocking her gently, while yelling, "Wake up, wake up!" Still, she did not rally.

He kicked at the doors from inside. Frozen tight. There was no other choice. He'd have to pull her through the rear window. It would be clumsy, but he would have to try. Although dead weight, she didn't compare to the calves he wrestled.

After several attempts, he succeeded. Hoping he hadn't hurt her too badly with his tugging, he managed to hoist her up into the tractor. He removed his jacket wrapping it gently around her. Leaning over he put his head on the young woman's chest. There was still a faint heartbeat. Pulling his gloves off, he placed his fingers against her wrist feeling for a pulse, frantically searching several spots. Not finding one, he moved to her carotid artery. There it was, albeit weak.

Could he get her to the clinic in time? Newcastle's clinic was thirty-five miles south. Fifty-seven miles to the regional hospital in Rapid City. The tractor was slow going. Hurry was out of the question. No sense calling an ambulance; they'd never make it up the road in this weather. All he could do would be to keep on a steady course and hope for the best.

At that moment, Kyle Fisher approached from plowing his section of road. Quaid waved him down and hollered out in passing, "Got an unconscious woman here. Is the road clear to town?"

"Can't say. I know Wade Bishop just finished his section when I started back. "What's wrong with her? Anything I can do?" He leaned out of the cab to get a better look. Steam puffed from his mouth like cigarette smoke in the cold mountain air.

"Not sure. Could be CO poisoning. Dumb broad left her motor running."

"I'll call in to the clinic and let 'em know you're on your way in."

"Thanks, Kyle." Waving each other off, Quaid sighed relief knowing the road was clear. Wade Bishop was the last rancher on the route. From his place, the county would have the road cleared into Newcastle. He might make better time than originally anticipated. The warmth of the cab brought a faint odor of urine. He glanced over at the limp, cyanotic woman noticing the wet pants. Losing control of her body functions was bad. He hoped he wouldn't pull into the clinic with a dead body. As the heavy machinery rolled down the road, he glanced at her from time to time wondering who she was. He knew most everyone in the area but didn't recollect seeing her face before.

7

Sure enough, Kyle Fisher had kept his word. No cars lined the parking lot, but as he pulled into the clinic, Doctor Dunacker stood waiting by the door in the reception area.

As Quaid opened the cab door, he heard Dunacker's voice. "What you got here? We've cancelled all appointments due to the weather. You're just lucky I live in town and can be on call for emergencies. Here, let me give you a hand."

They lifted the limp woman from the tractor and carried her into an examination room laying her on a table. Wanting firsthand information on her condition, Quaid hesitated leaving. He paced nervously around the small exam room, digging his hands in and out of his pockets.

"Fisher said you found her in a running vehicle. Possible CO poisoning. What's the story?" Dunacker asked glancing over the young woman's body. He frowned, placing his stethoscope to her heart. "Might not be too promising a future for her. Could be brain damage. Nerve damage. Any rallying since you found her?"

"No, sir." Quaid almost choked on the words. "Is she. . .?" He'd seen plenty of death in the ranch animals, but other than his aged parents, he hadn't witnessed a human death. Although she was a stranger, he hoped she didn't die.

"Why don't you go out into the waiting room, Quaid." Seconds later, Dunacker returned his attention to the patient.

Ill at ease being shut out from her prognosis, Quaid paced the perimeter of the room. Ethically, he should return to his road plowing, yet curiosity held him there. Maybe waiting a few more minutes wouldn't hurt anything. Most folks would know the roads were closed and his chances of finding another stranded motorist were slight. He slung his lanky frame into a chair, grabbed a magazine, flipping through it without really looking at it.

Quaid Kincaid had spent his whole life in the Rocky Mountains. A storm like this was nothing new. People just prepared themselves ahead of time. If you had to travel, you made sure you stocked your vehicle with warm clothing, blankets, a shovel, flares, an emergency first-aid kit, a couple cans of beans and some candy bars. Only greenhorns or reckless people challenged Mother Nature. Which one was she? In the past he had rescued his share of foolhardy travelers, although none had been in this woman's condition. Most people had more sense than to go out on a day like today. What had she been thinking? Didn't she listen to the radio like everyone else? It was just common sense to listen to the weather and ag report first thing each morning. If she had, she'd known the mountain passes closed hours ago.

"What? You're still here?" Dunacker walked out into the reception area removing his stethoscope from around his neck stuffing it into the pocket of his lab coat.

Quaid rose. "She going to make it?"

"Yes, yes, I think so. I have her on oxygen. As soon as the roads clear, I'll need to transport her to the regional hospital in Rapid. There may be damage I can't ascertain. These are limited facilities."

Quaid nodded, disappointed he wouldn't know her outcome. He couldn't wait for the ambulance, nor could he follow them to the hospital. However, he could follow up with a phone call. Instantly the futility of the situation struck him as he realized he didn't even know her name.

"Someone you know, Quaid?" Dunacker looked at him intermittently while making notes on a chart.

He looked down at his feet, holding his hat in his hands in front of him. He mumbled, "Nope."

"Name? Any ID?"

"I don't know. I didn't think to look. Just grabbed her and . . . . "

9

"Hmm. Jane Doe. Well, go home then. I'm sure she's going to live, although I can't say what her quality of life will be. Nothing more we can do. I'll stay with her until we can transfer her."

All the way home, Quaid wondered who she could be. When he spied the ice-encrusted vehicle again, he stopped to look for a purse, vehicle registration, anything that would give a clue to her identity or where she was from. Searching the seats, he found her purse wedged under the passenger seat. He pulled it out and then stood alongside her vehicle riffling through her belongings.

"Page Chandling," he read, looking at the driver's license. The woman in the picture was not the pale, lifeless form he had pulled from the vehicle. Bright, blue eyes sparkled in a flawless complexion. Long, shoulder length hair with just a flip on the ends framed her oval face. He read the rest of the info: "5'5", weight132, expiration date 7-21-08." It was an Illinois license. He walked behind the vehicle to take down the plate number for the police. Wyoming plates? Newcomers didn't need to change their driver's license until they'd been in the state for a year. Did that mean she was a newcomer? Or were they stolen plates? No, she seemed too innocent for that. Or maybe not. Maybe she was on the run and just decided to end it all.

He noted how close the car sat on the edge of the precipice. Only a small margin of snow had kept her from sliding over. Assessing the damage, he ascertained she'd need a new rear window where snow and sleet filled in the back seat. It was a wet mess now, but that could dry out especially if he put the car in his barn. Vacillating whether to tow the vehicle to his ranch or have the police impound it, he decided they would be busy enough with in-town accidents. Attaching a tow strap to the lower control arm, he jerked the Taurus out of the banked snow before heading home, all the while wondering why the pretty lady had sat in her car with the motor running. Stupidity? Suicide? Or just accidental.

CHAPTER TWO

"Aren't you scared to travel so far all alone?"

"What if you have a blowout?"

"Hot damn, girl, go for it. Maybe you'll meet a randy cowboy that wants to buck your bod."

Who was saying those things? Voices whirled through her head. Was she dreaming? Page groaned. Unable to open her eyes, she drifted in and out of consciousness.

"Good for you, honey. It's about time you left that sonofabitch."

Who'd said that? Kailee, in bookkeeping.

"Kailee?" she murmured. Ever so slowly, Page opened her eyes, then closed them; she felt groggy and very strange. But she remembered who the sonofabitch was. Michael. Her ex.

Rumors of Michael's infidelity had filtered through the office reaching everyone's ears but hers. Although she surmised Michael had been cheating, she did not want to believe he would demand fidelity and honesty from her and not practice it himself. Nor did she have the guts to confront him or catch him in the act. His explosive temper would only result in another beating. Rather, she suffered in silence, continuing to be the good, faithful wife until that day when she opened the front door only to be served divorce papers.

Divorced now, his parting words in the courtroom rang in her ears haunting her: "You'll never be out of my sight, never out of my life." It made no sense to her. Yet years of being controlled and the object of his irrational wrath, she was still living with fear.

Determined to distance herself from him after the trial, she impulsively decided to change her life. Only a few hours after leaving the courtroom, she threw caution to the wind. Jumping into her Taurus with a few personal items and Sam, she headed west, her head filled with cowboys, mountain men, and pioneer women from her favorite novels. Strong where she was weak, she figured that if she placed herself in a rugged, unforgiving land like Wyoming, she would deal with the same hardships as her forbearers; in time, emulating them would change her into the tough survivalist she yearned to be—a self-reliant woman needing no man.

Michael. Leave me alone. . . No! No Michael! The next moment, she was floating on clouds again.

Hours later, she awoke with her head feeling like a big cotton ball, her vision blurry, and a jittery sensation like an electric shock coursing through her. *Can't breathe, can't . . . suffocating.* She grabbed at her face, pulling away an oxygen mask. No sooner had she pulled it away than strange, tingling spasms went through her. Her chest hurt as she breathed. And her head! Her head felt like it was doing the Macarena. Letting it drop back in place, her head lolled to the left. A strange man stretched out in a recliner near her bedside. The soles of his dirty cowboy boots propped themselves on the foot of her bed. As her eyes came into focus, she moved them upward. A lanky, blue jean clad male wearing a pale, blue western shirt with pearl snaps greeted her. A black cowboy hat covered his face. *Who?*

13

The stranger flung his feet off the bed, righted himself in the chair, grabbed his hat off, and held it in front of himself, "You're awake."

Duh! "Who are you?" Her voice sounded wobbly and loud to her own ears and she wondered if it sounded that way to him. Still groggy, she fluttered her eyelids open and close.

"Quaid Kincaid, ma'am. I'm the one that found you."

"Found me? Where?" Her speech sounded thick and sluggish. He was standing beside the bed looking down at her. Her eyes scanned from his chest to his face. Whoa, momma! Have I died and gone to heaven? What a hottie! He could be Allan Jackson's twin.

"In a snow bank on the Sundance county road, ma'am."

Always a sucker for a good-looking man she stared at him, hearing the words but not really listening as her pulse raced, pounding in her ears. *If this is what doctors are like in the West, he can treat me anytime.*

"Not a real smart thing to do. . . "

What is he talking about? She tried to make some sense out of what she heard. *Sundance road?* Closing her eyes, she willed the pain in her head to go away. The next time she opened her eyes, she looked around the hospital room. *Wait! A snow bank.* She seemed to recall driving. But what had happened?

The cowboy was still there, pacing around the foot of the bed as he spoke. Her eyes followed him back and forth. *Hold still!* When he did pause, she studied the angular planes of his face, sunken cheeks, deep-set chocolate eyes, his sun bronzed skin, the Robert Redford style haircut. He ran long, thin fingers through his short brown hair flicking it to the side, before nervously worrying the brim of the Stetson.

14

". . . leaving the motor running . . . only a fool would do that."

What? Is he calling me a fool? . . . The motor running? Rising up on one elbow she was about to give him a piece of her mind when tiny fireworks ignited behind her eyes before shrouding over into a sea of blackness. The room darkened and fell away as his voice drowned in the darkening depths.

Later that day, she awoke once again. The room was empty. Her head felt a little clearer. The pain not as acute. The oxygen mask was gone. Her bed had been cranked up to a near upright position and an aide was pulling the portable table across her bed. In seconds, the aide laid a tray on the table before leaving the room. Smelling food, she didn't care if hospital food did get a bad rap, she was starved. How long had it been since she'd ate? But more importantly, she looked around. Where was the cowboy with the soft chocolate eyes? Had she been dreaming? She chided herself. *Stop getting carried away. Handsome men are trouble.* She tilted her head, sniffing. *Wasn't that a whiff of aftershave in the air? Where was he?*

The next forty-eight hours nurses, doctors and a psychologist asked her repeatedly what she remembered, what her name was, did she know where she was, on and on until she questioned *their* sanity. Finally, she must have passed their tests. Her doctor stood before her now at her bedside preparing to release her, provided there was someone to look after her for the next three or four days.

"Let me just change some of this paperwork. You were admitted as Jane Doe, Ms. Chandling. Since, Mr. Kincaid has notified us of your proper name, address, and such. Is there a next of kin or someone you'd like—?"

"No!" She didn't mean to be so abrupt, but all she could think of was Michael knowing of her whereabouts and that sent panic through her.

15

"I'm sorry, but carbon monoxide poisoning is a serious thing; it can have some far reaching effects. You're lucky Mr. Kincaid found you when he did or you'd be in the morgue," the red headed, overweight doctor told her. "You may still have moments of disorientation; you could stumble and fall. You could have any number of accidents due to nerve damage. You need to have someone around for the next few days in case there are side effects." He jotted a few notes on her chart just as Quaid walked in the room.

Her breath caught. It's him. The chocolate eyed cowboy. He isn't a doctor after all.

"Speak of the devil. How're ya, Quaid?" The two men shook hands like old friends.

What had the doctor said a moment ago? Kincaid gave him her name, address? How? My purse! Her eyes searched the room. "Where is my purse?"

"I'm afraid I took it to the ranch for safekeeping. Didn't think you'd need it in here," Quaid said.

She gasped. She still carried a card listing Michael as a contact in case of an accident. *Oh, my God, what if they called Michael? What will he do? Fly out?*

"Ms. Chandling? Are you all right? Tell me what's going on," said the doctor noticing her sudden distress.

"Huh? Oh, uh, nothing. I guess. Just flashes of things going through my head."

"Pain? Remembering things?" He studied her face.

"No. No pain." She shook her head.

"Hear you can go home today. Figured you'd need a ride," the slim, brown-eyed cowboy said, strolling to her bedside with a paper bag in his hands.

"I can drive my car. Besides, I don't know you," she said warily.

"That might be a tad difficult, ma'am. Your car is out at my ranch."

His ranch? Why is my car at his ranch? "Then I guess I'm stuck here. I have to have a babysitter according to the doctor and I don't know a soul in Wyoming." *Oops! Why did I say that? Is that an invitation putting me at risk? Wyoming!* She had said Wyoming. At least she knew where she was. Bits and pieces of her memory seemed to be returning.

"I ain't one for babysitting, but I can take you out to the ranch and have Kait look after you," Quaid said, continuing the conversation.

So, this dreamy, slightly bow-legged cowboy is a rancher. How lucky can I get? My first cowboy. A second of pleasure swept through her followed by a tug of attraction. Instantaneously, as if not allowed to entertain such thoughts, her brain sent a warning: *Forget it Page. Men are scum. Besides, he's married. On the other hand, if Michael does come looking for me, would he look for me at a ranch?* She knew she had to stop looking over her shoulder expecting Michael to be there. Yet she knew him better than anyone did. With his money and connections, little was out of his reach or control. Nor were his threats idle. Michael was dangerous. His favorite saying popped into her head: "That's not a threat, that's a promise."

Quaid, on the other hand, seemed nice if first impressions could be counted on. He seemed well mannered, but terse. But why would a total stranger be so concerned about her? Was that natural? Somehow, it seemed safer when she had assumed he was a western doctor. Now she wasn't sure. Now he was just a cowboy. A man. A strange man. Obviously someone she would have to deal with if she hoped to leave the hospital and get her car back.

She watched him while the doctor spoke. It appeared he was a no nonsense rancher by his demeanor. He didn't smile at all. Although he appeared quite dour, she found him incredibly attractive. So much so, she mused what it would be like to have a relationship with him. But more importantly, what type of temperament did he have? Would he volatile like Michael? No, he must be sensitive and caring to be so willing to help an absolute stranger.

Just as quickly her thoughts changed. Michael had also been incredibly handsome, charming her, making her believe he was sensitive and caring. It wasn't until after she had fallen hard and fast his true nature came out. After being the victim of his abuse, she swore she would never do that again, never fall for a smooth talker again. She had resolved to keep her guard up at all times. Yet here she was already slipping up and finding herself attracted to this strange cowboy who was offering to take her to his ranch. She told herself she didn't know Mr. Kincaid from a mesquite bush and she'd better stay wary.

"No, thank you. I wouldn't want to impose." Why would he invite a total stranger to his ranch? And what was his wife going to say about him bringing me there?

As if reading her mind, the doctor interjected, "You'll be in good hands, Ms Chandling. I've known Quaid and Kait for several years now. In fact, I've patched him up more times than I care to recall."

"No imposition. Just a body helping a body. It's called hospitality out here. Why don't you get dressed and I'll pick you up out front? I almost forgot. These here are some of Kait's clothes and boots. Maybe they'll fit. You sure weren't dressed for Wyoming weather." He laid the paper bag on the bed and turned to go.

Still unsettled whether to trust this stranger, yet wanting to get out of the hospital, curiosity got the best of her; she opened the paper bag. Inside she found a pair of jeans, a sweater and a pair of galoshes. On the very bottom was a new package of underwear size 6. *His wife's clothes? What if they didn't fit?*

Reluctant, yet swayed by the doctor's remark, she acquiesced. When the men left the room, she pulled the items out of the bag and tried them on. Amazingly, they fit, although the sweater was a little tight. Still scared at the thought of going off to god knows where with a strange man, she weighed the pros and cons. Con, he could kidnap her, rape her, leave her in the sagebrush. Who knows what could happen. Pro, the doctor wouldn't release her into danger, would he? Secretly, she felt thrilled to be going to a real working ranch; her thoughts ran rampant. It would be just like the movies—horses and cattle, cowboys in chaps toting gun belts, whisky-drinking men stretched out in the bunkhouse. How exciting. She'd have spaces to explore, prairies to hike, wildlife to encounter. It was everything she wanted—adventure, narrow escapes, learning to live by her wits. She brightened, stiffening her resolve as she pulled the boots on. She just hoped Mr. Kincaid's wife understood.

As she waited for the nurse to escort her out in a wheelchair, something nagged at her; was there something she was neglecting? Unable to put it together, she proceeded to argue with the nurse about walking out on her own volition. It was a losing battle; the nurse sat her down in the wheelchair and started down the hall to the elevator.

Waiting at the exit doors, a little black and white tabby with a white streak down its nose peered in through the glass, then darted away. She loved cats. *A yellow tabby. I have a cat or at least had one at one time. But when was that?* It seemed recent, yet if that were true, where was it? *Is this poor little thing a stray? If so, I'll adopt it and Sammy will have a playmate. Sammy. That was the name of* her *cat!* Cold air smacked her as the wide sliding glass doors of the hospital exit opened and she shivered. Maybe the cold air will clear my thoughts. She peered around for the tabby, but it was nowhere to be seen.

A beat up powder blue and what used to be white, now yellow cream, pick-up truck rolled up to the entrance. Quaid jumped from the driver's side and came around the vehicle opening the passenger door. He went to where she sat in a wheelchair and offered his hand to her.

"I don't need your help. I'm fine," she said brusquely, eschewing his hand and rising from the wheelchair.

Narrowing his eyes, he set his jaw, hardened his face. He stepped back, withdrawing. "Fine. Get in."

"This?" She looked askance at the rusting door panels, the dents, the dings, the broken headlight.

"What's wrong with this?" he challenged, standing by the opened door.

"I thought you cowboys all had new Fords and Chevys," she replied, eyeing the mélange of papers and paraphernalia covering the seat and dash.

"Lady, you watch too much TV. Are you going to get in or do I have to put you in? I have work to do."

Impatient, he was now getting surly. It reminded her of Michael. Feeling apprehensive, she said, "I've changed my mind. I'll take a cab home."

"A what?" he asked flabbergasted, staring at her, shaking his head.

"A cab. A taxi. Now just go," she urged, shooing him away.

"First off, we don't have any of those things. Secondly, I only agreed to this because you're not a native. You don't seem to know where you live, so until you do I guess you're stuck with me. Since I know what it's like not to have money to pay bills, and by the looks of the bills in your purse, you need all the help you can get. And you could show a little gratitude while you're at it," he added before grabbing her hand, guiding her into the truck.

"How dare you!" Indignant at having her personal possessions pawed through, she yanked her hand away. Then realizing she had no other choice, she belligerently climbed in his truck. Handsome or not, she was right, this cowboy was bad news.

*　*　*　*

As Quaid drove through Rapid City, out into the rural communities on the way back to Sundance, memories flickered in and out of her head. Several inches of snow covered the land and large drifts bowed wire fence lines. Four-foot drifts lined the roadbed. Flashes of farmland, small towns, men talking corn and hog belly prices skipped through her mind. Iowa! Prairies, the graceful grasses swaying back and forth like a hula skirt, piercing sun. South Dakota! But it hadn't been winter at that time. When had it snowed? She remembered eating in small ma and pa type restaurants where everyone knew everyone. Not like Leitchfield where people didn't even grunt a good morning to you. Leitchfield. She could remember her old hometown. Her memory was coming back.

"What brings you to Wyoming?" he asked, keeping his eyes on the road, although only two or three cars had passed them.

Page, stilled peeved at his going through her purse, hesitated wondering how candid to be. Could she trust this man? "Moving." Instantly she berated herself for her blatant honesty. He didn't need to know the truth. Especially if he'd contacted her ex. She should control herself better; her naïve trust and openness would get her into trouble someday.

"Newcastle," she said as they passed a mileage sign.

"You . . . know someone . . . in Newcastle?" he drew the words out cautiously.

She thought. "Um, no. I don't think so. It just sounds familiar." Something about the name picked at her making her uneasy. If only she could remember. She fidgeted in the seat as she watched the scenery fly by.

Quaid pulled off on County Road Seven. At first, Page thought the territory looked familiar but then one stretch of prairie ran into another and another and soon they all looked the same. As they reached the ranch, she looked up to read the overhanging crossbar: DOUBLE K. *A middle name perhaps? Or what was his wife's name? Kait. Kait Kincaid. The ranch must belong to her.* Turning into the drive, the vehicle jostled about as they ran over tubular rolls of steel.

"What's that?" she asked grasping for the grab handle.

"Cattle guard. Most ranches have them. The cattle don't like walking over them; they're afraid of falling through the slats."

"Oh." She tucked the information away in her memory. "Oh, look!" Excited, she pointed out the window.

Accustomed to the sight, he showed no excitement. "Mule deer," he said as the herd ran parallel to the vehicle.

Flashes of animals came to mind. More images. A zoo. Memories were rushing in faster than she could assimilate. She watched as mile after mile of pristine snow like a warm fleece blanket ran to the horizon, stretching far as the eye could see, running to the edges of the distant mountains. She loved snow! Being a Mid-Westerner, accustomed to four seasons, she was most partial to fall and winter. She loved cool weather, the raucous fall colors, apple orchards, the smell of road-kill apples tangy with fermentation, pumpkins glowing like orange moons in the twilight, harvesting nuts, free for the picking. A roaring bonfire on a crisp, cold Illinois night. Usually around October, the weather ran to rainy, gloomy days accentuating her seasonal affective disorder, nevertheless she loved a rip-roaring thunderstorm with thunder booming and lightening crashing. Yet on the whole she preferred sunny days and today the sun was accommodating her, even reflecting off the snow.

"Sure is bright out here," she said shading her eyes with her hands. "I'll have to get some sunglasses," she said, hoping for a little conversation. It had been a long silent ride.

Quaid grunted.

He stopped before a modest bungalow. "This is it."

She stared crestfallen. *This is a ranch house?* What about all those gorgeous log homes with stone fireplaces she seen in home magazines and assumed all rich ranchers had? This was nothing but a shabby bungalow with a couple of additions on it. As she stepped out of the truck two dogs came bounding towards her. Reaching down to pet one, it growled at her. She jerked her hand back and danced lightly in the snow hoping it wouldn't bite her.

"Blue heelers, they won't hurt you," he said coming around from the other side of the truck. "They're used to chasing cattle. Anything that walks gets their attention." He gave a command and the dogs settled down to trot near his side. "Ol' Chester here might try nipping your ankles, but I've never known him to bite. Blue's younger, friskier." He ruffled the dogs' necks.

Page loved animals, but Chester and Blue made her nervous the way they kept sneaking up behind her, nipping at her heels. If she turned around to look at them, they would bound away only to return seconds later.

She reached out for the support pole on the porch; weathered, blistered paint flaked off into the snow. She avoided stepping on the riser; splintered, it looked like a beaver had been gnawing on it. When she stepped inside, her eyes had to adjust to the dark surroundings. Tacked to the picture window was an old Indian blanket. The wood floors were bare and worn. In the dim light she couldn't tell if the walls were—white, yellow, or gray. What a slob she thought looking around. Magazines and papers covered the tables, the couch, and the floor. Dirty coffee mugs and glasses were everywhere, on the floor, a windowsill, and lay overturned in chair seats. A discolored pillow and heavy wool horse blanket lay crumpled up on the sagging sofa. It looked like an elephant had sat on it. She sneezed as disturbed dust particles floated through the air. A bunch of leather stuff she only knew by the general term "tack" was lying around everywhere. And it smelled faintly like a barn.

She smiled weakly hoping her quarters would be cleaner and better than this. Quaid motioned to a room off the hallway. Disappointment followed as she stared. A flat pillow and a heavy fleece comforter with horses on it lie atop a lumpy looking mattress on a narrow single bed. A nightstand, vintage 1960, held an equally unattractive lamp. The scarred maple dresser with the large mirror over it looked crippled canting slightly on a bent leg. A single roller shade, yellowed with age, covered the one narrow window in the room.

Quaid pulled up the shade a bit letting some light into the room. "Don't get much company. It's clean though. You'll probably be so tired you won't even notice the lumps in the bed. I'll go round up an extra blanket."

Not wanting to appear ungracious, she gave him a gratuitous smile wishing she could have went to a motel. *Motel! Yes!* It was all coming back to her. She had been traveling. Heading for Wyoming. Upon her arrival, she had rented a motel room until she could find a job and save enough money for a more permanent home. But where was the motel? Was that why Newcastle had such a familiar ring? A second later, all the pieces jelled together and she realized the significance of the yellow tabby. *Sam must be in Newcastle at the motel! Poor Sammy. He must be starving.* She had to find her car and get back to Sam. Now, if she could just remember the name of the motel.

CHAPTER THREE

"Here's another blanket. Gets cold at night." Quaid dropped the blanket on the bed. Then turning to go, added, "Might as well make yourself useful . . . come out to the stable."

She followed behind him. "The stable? I thought I was a guest."

He pivoted to face her. "Look, I've lost a lot of time looking after you. Time I should have been checking cattle, mucking stables, oiling tack."

Whoa! What happened between the hospital and the ranch? "Well, who asked you to?" she spouted, puzzled and annoyed by his abrupt change of demeanor. No sooner were the words out of her mouth than she regretted them. It wasn't like her to be blatant or rude. Now she worried about how he would react. She knew how Michael would have reacted. Her words would have set off a barrage of demeaning abuse. Would Quaid be the same? Was she treading dangerous ground?

He heaved a heavy sigh. "Well, okay, I guess I can manage without you tonight. But if you're going to be spending time here, you need to get acquainted with things, the animals and all. I'll be in after sundown sometime. Why don't you rustle up something for us to eat? You can cook, can't you?"

How dare he order me around? I'm a guest.

"Uh, just what is after sundown? Is that six-ish? Seven? Later? I-I don't eat that late. And what do you mean you can do without me tonight?" she asked. Nervous thoughts popped into her head. Was he suggesting something sexual?

"Just keep it warm. It means I'll be here when I get here. . . . as far as the other, first thing you learn out here is everybody pulls their own weight. . . . didn't think you were going to some fancy B&B, did you?" He scowled.

"Well, I don't know what I expected." *But certainly something better than this!* Compliant, she followed him to the kitchen wondering where Mrs. Kincaid was. When would she be home? "I'll see what I can do." Then testing the waters, she drew herself up and with more bravado than she felt, added, "Tomorrow I'm out of here. I can manage very well on my own."

Bracing herself for an argument, he merely turned his back to her, opened the back door, pushed the screen door open, and walked away saying, "Uh huh. Everything takes time to heal."

Page gritted her teeth. *He's just going to go off and leave me? And what is that remark supposed to mean? Ugh, he was irritating.*

Once he was out of sight, Page wandered through the small house. The rooms were small and painted in nondescript beige or maybe it was aged white. The sheen was long gone from the wooden floors, and the throw rugs were full of dog fur looking like they hadn't been washed since being laid down. She stuck her head in the bathroom. It was decently clean with the exception of whisker shavings that had missed the wastebasket. His bedroom was a hodge-podge of tack and clothing lying around. The bed was unmade. Familiarizing herself with the floor plan and contents, she wandered back out to the kitchen and ruffled through a stack of papers eventually finding a telephone directory. She looked up motels then ran her finger up and down the list.

"The Wagon Wheel Inn. That sounds about right." She dialed the number, stopped, and hung up. She hadn't registered Sammy. If the manager hadn't already thrown him out, he certainly would when she called. The thought of Sammy being tossed outdoors to wander strange streets made her edgy as a cat in heat.

She went in the living room and turned on the TV. A snowy picture of a news program came on. Flipping through the channels, she found one other station and it too did not come in clearly. Unable to enjoy it, she turned it back off and picked up a magazine, flipping through the pages. Never having horses, the text was too technical for her; she quickly laid it back down. Boredom and tiredness struck her; she decided to lie down until it was time to make dinner.

At five-thirty, she rose and went out to the small kitchen to prepare their meal. Page, having studied interior design at an earlier point in her life, recognized the Youngstown metal cabinets in the small L-shaped kitchen. The sink was an old white porcelain single basin. A turquoise Frigidaire colored the otherwise stark room. It was so different from her stainless steel high-tech kitchen back in Leitchfield and so much more crowded as she tried to find enough space on the counter to work.

A search of the refrigerator revealed hot dogs, hamburger and beer. The freezer had several wrapped packages, but judging how long it would take to thaw, she nixed that idea. Settling on something quick and fast, she pulled the ground beef out of the refrigerator and set it on the counter before perusing the cupboards. Beans, beans, and more beans. And one box of mac and cheese. That would have to do.

A few hours later, Quaid sauntered in discarding his outerwear on a peg in the mudroom. He sat down at the kitchen table, heaped with a mass of bills, papers, magazines, empty sacks, nuts, bolts, pencils, and pens, while waiting to be served.

Page laid a plate with a hamburger and macaroni and cheese in front of him.

He peered down at the plate, a disgruntled look on his face. "This the best you could do?"

"Well, excussssssssssse me. Maybe you should just make your own meals."

"Kinda testy, aren't you? Where's the rest of it?"

"The rest of what?" she asked, despising his surliness.

"You're giving me one hamburger and a couple spoonfuls of mac and cheese? I'm not on a diet. And where's yours?"

Page glared at him. What a boor. "I've already ate. I told you I don't eat this late. What do you want to drink?"

"Anything I can have more than one of."

She set two longnecks in front of him.

"Could you open those for me?" He peered at her.

She pursed her lips and stormed over to the silverware drawer to find a bottle opener. *I'm not his damn servant. I had enough of that with Michael.* Nevertheless, she popped the tops and plopped herself down in a chair like an errant child that was about to be scolded.

Several minutes passed in silence before the tension resolved itself.

"Uh. . . Quaid?" She waited for his acknowledgement. When she had his attention, she continued. "I need to get to the Wagon Wheel Inn. In Newcastle."

"The Wagon Wheel? Why?" He stopped shoveling the macaroni around on his plate and looked up at her.

She hesitated. "Sam's there."

28

He jerked upright at full attention. A look of distaste hardened his face.

"Sam? I thought you didn't know anyone here."

"I-I don't. You see, I came here with Sam and—"

"Jesus Christ, lady." He jumped out of the kitchen chair and paced, running his hands through his hair nervously. "You could have told me you were married or had a boyfriend. The roads are in no condition to drive or I'd tell you to get out right now. Snow's blowin' and driftin' again, so I guess you'll have to spend the night. I don't reckon this Sam character could get here until after the road's plowed in the morning anyhow. Christ almighty, I don't want no trouble. Why in hell didn't you tell me about Sam?"

"But Sam isn't—" Cowering at his explosiveness, she felt it best not to say more.

"Oh, shit. I'm. . ." He rubbed his fingers over a heavy five o-clock shadow. "Damn it all. I don't want to hear anymore." He pointed a long slender finger at her. "Tomorrow morning you're out of here." He got up, threw his outerwear on again and stormed outside.

Uneasy she could not get back to Newcastle until morning, she busied herself drawing water in the kitchen sink for the dishes. She quickly rinsed out the glasses, coffee cups and plates they had used and a few pieces of silverware while she tried to figure out Quaid's angry outburst. If he'd only let her explain maybe he wouldn't be so angry. He sure had a short fuse. She would be glad to be gone. Sammy's company was totally preferable to Quaid's.

Finished with that task, she whirled around to view the helter-skelter magazines and coffee cups throughout the house. Collecting all the cups she could find, she then proceeded to wash them. Engrossed in stacking magazines she startled when she didn't hear him come up behind her.

"Leave my stuff alone. If I wanted a maid I'd hire one." He came over to her and removed the magazines she

29

was holding, throwing them down haphazardly, before walking over to a roll-top desk and sitting down.

She stopped in her tracks wanting to tell him she thought he was an ungrateful pig. However, as a guest, she was on his turf. She should probably say nothing. Besides, it would probably set him off again. Deciding she didn't need any more abuse, she decided to be just as short and rude as he was. "Sorry. Goodnight." She went into the bedroom shutting the door with more force than necessary.

"'night," he said, without bothering to look up from the stack of papers before him.

Within the folds of the blanket he'd given her, he'd tucked one of his flannel shirts to sleep in and some wool socks in case her feet got cold. With the door closed the heat didn't seem to be circulating and the room was chilly. Wasting no time, she undressed and put his shirt on inhaling the fresh laundry scent. The wool socks were too big and kept creeping down her feet with each step. Hastily, she drew back the covers and got in the bed with the cold sheets sending a shiver down her spine. Turning off the nightlight, she pulled the heavy blanket up around her ears.

Page tossed and turned in the lumpy bed. No matter how hard she tried, sleep would not come. Lying in the dark, her thoughts bounced back and forth between Quaid's irrational irritation and Sammy. Sammy probably thought she had deserted him. Grateful the ad had jogged her memory she murmured, *Hang in there Sammy, mama's coming soon.*

The longer she lie there, the more she realized she was feeling normal again. Just knowing she hadn't experienced any of the after effects the doctor warned her of heightened her sense of security. Now if she could just get through the night.

She could hear Quaid in the adjacent room shuffling papers and talking on the phone. Was she safe being alone in the house with him? Where was what's her name? Kait.

Why didn't she come home? Wasn't Quaid concerned about her?

The aromatic smell of brewing coffee awakened her. Looking at the cracked, plastic alarm clock on the nightstand, she groaned. *Who gets up at four a.m.?* It was still dark outside. Flipping on the light, the first thing she noticed was the door. It was open! She was sure she had closed it. Throwing back the blankets, she found the room warmer than when she had went to bed yet still drafty in her scanty nightclothes. She plodded to the kitchen to find Quaid pouring coffee and munching on donut holes. With the anger of the previous night dissipated, she greeted him in a half-yawn, "Morning."

Pivoting on his heels, and then stared. "Good Mornin'."

She noticed his gaze pinpointed on her breasts as his eyes traveled down her body, then back up, making her feel naked and exposed.

"Coffee?" He held out an empty cup.

She nodded assent, shivered, and sat down in one of the chrome and red vinyl chairs, rising and sitting uneasily as the cold materials touched her warm flesh.

"The pot's on the counter. Help yourself." He walked out of the room.

Incensed by his rudeness, she got up and poured herself a cup, then opened drawers until she found a spoon. She spent a moment searching for the cream and sugar before discovering it was on a lazy-susan on the table. Just as she went to sit down, Quaid came back.

"I washed your clothes last night. And, I forgot to tell you if you close the door, it gets cold as a barn in there. You were asleep, so I opened it before I went to bed. Here's my robe. It'll keep you warm."

Huh! What a dichotomy he is.

31

She graciously accepted the robe from him wrapping it around herself. "Thank you." Immediately the warmth seeped into her along with the subtle scent of some masculine fragrance. What was with this guy? Hadn't he told her to get out? Why was he being so nice this morning? What kind of Jekyll and Hyde was she mixed up with now?

Quaid sat across from her, looking over his coffee cup observing her. Other than Kaitlin, it had been years since a woman had been at the ranch. Years since he'd seen a woman scantily dressed. His testosterone rising, he had to keep telling himself she was sick and recuperating. *Sam must be a lucky man.* Knowing she had a man friend, there wasn't much point in starting a conversation with her, much less anything else. It was the anything else he was trying to control this morning. He wished now he hadn't loaned her his shirt to sleep in. It barely covered her essentials, resting high on her thighs. The top two buttons were undone and her cleavage was showing through the plackets of the shirt. He couldn't help but see the rounded firmness of her breasts as she leaned over the table to reach the cream and sugar. Didn't she know what a sight like that did to a guy? Happy to oblige her with his robe, it didn't help the growing feeling in his groin. When she looked at him, he diverted his gaze.

Moments later, unable to stay silent, he broke in with an impersonal question. "See you got an Illinois license, but a Wyoming license plate. How'd that come about?" He sipped his coffee.

"How do you know that?" she asked, as she dipped her lips to the rim of the steaming coffee mug.

"I rescued you, remember? When the hospital needed a name, I had to go through your purse. Sorry, I know they're sacrosanct to ladies. Your driver's license is from Illinois." He was full of questions but decided it was futile asking them in light of her commitment to Sam.

"Where's Kait?" she asked looking around, pulling the robe tighter around herself.

At that instant, the phone rang. Quaid, with a mouth full of donut, hesitated and motioned for her to answer it.

"Kincaid's." Like a deer caught in headlights, the voice on the other end made her freeze, turning her pale. She hung up. "That was Kait. She'll be here in a few minutes." Aware of her disarray, she grabbed her clean clothes he had laid out on the kitchen table, hurried back to the bedroom and dressed. When Page returned to the kitchen, he was donning a jacket and boots.

"Wait! Where's my car? Keys?" she said, her high pitched tone disclosing her distress.

"Car's in the barn. Keys here on the peg by the door. You ain't plannin' on takin' off are you?" He studied her.

"I have to. Besides, that's what you wanted. Remember?" She grabbed the keys from the peg and busted out the door.

"Hey, you don't even have a coat on, you crazy greenhorn." Damn! He didn't have time to argue with her. It had snowed again during the night and he'd have to plow again. He wished Kaitlin had been there when he first brought Page to the ranch. If only he'd thought to call Kaitlin before Page's release from the hospital. She could have been there by now.

Kaitlin had to come from Aladdin, about thirty-five miles east. Although they were exceptionally close for brother and sister, Quaid was rather negligent on his part. He usually waited for his sister to check in with him, rather than vice-versa, only calling her when he needed help. And boy, did he need help. Reminded by the doctor's words that Page needed supervision for a few days, he was nonplussed what to do. Should he stop her? Or let her run to Sam? *Kaitlin, where the hell are you?.*

Going out the door, he recalled how resistant Page had been to come to the ranch and now how eager to get away. "Hells bells, if that's what she wants, so be it," he muttered, but his words evaporated in the cold Wyoming morning.

Apparently, she had fallen asleep thinking Kait would arrive home during the night. Over coffee, she thought maybe Kait was sleeping in late. With her head clearer than the night previous, she felt progressively better, the effects of the carbon monoxide leaving her system.

Still scared to divulge much personal information to Quaid, she'd clammed up at the breakfast table. Why did he need to know about her? She hated interrogation. It made her feel like she was back with Michael. Trapped and afraid. Afraid of saying something wrong, of saying too much, not enough, saying something that would set him off. It was better to be evasive and quiet although this strange cowboy intrigued her.

Not until the phone rang and she heard Kait's voice did she realize she had spent the entire night alone with Kait's husband. A chill of fear coursed through her wondering what Kait would think, say, or do. The situation was too intense. All she could think of was getting away fast before Kait showed up. Confrontation was just too scary.

Trudging through the snow, her sneakers were wet and her feet cold before reaching the barn. Coatless, she shivered, realizing she'd been stupid to burst out the door without the protective clothing he'd brought her in the hospital. She tugged and tugged at the door, cursing under her breath, but the night's moisture had made the door's runner icy and unmovable. Exerting all her energy, she kept at the task until Chester and Blue came bounding through the snow in her direction. Wary, she jumped back hoping they would not attack. When they stood nearby wagging their tails, she relaxed and resumed tugging at the door again. It moved a couple of inches. Sweating from exertion and anxiety, her heart pounding in flight mode, she froze, arrested, when she heard a melodious woman's voice.

"Can I help you with that?"

Caught like a thief, Page whirled around to face a stunning brunette. A petite woman with soft brown eyes and long chestnut hair pulled back in a ponytail smiled and reached out a hand. "I'm Kaitlin Kincaid. Quaid's sister."

The woman's words didn't register at first. Stunned, Page groveled for words, ". . . sorry . . . an accident. Quaid brought me here . . . need to go home."

"I know," Kait said in dulcet tones, noticing the desperation clouding Page's face.

Quaid caught up with them and made introductions. "Page Chandling, my sister Kaitlin, Kait, Page."

Sister. He said sister, she said sister. Not wife. The tension in Page's body oozed away realizing she was not confronting his wife.

Kaitlin said, "You sure are a greenhorn. You're not dressed for Wyoming. C'mon in the house. I'm not much of a cook, but I can rustle up some eggs and toast. I'll stick a towel in the microwave to warm your feet. They must be half frozen in those things." She stood looking down at Page's white canvas sneakers.

Nice. She's nice. Then she thought about Quaid's threat. She remembered Sammy. "No, you don't understand. I have to go. Sam. . . ."

"C'mon. You can tell me all about Sam over breakfast." Kaitlin reached out to hold Page's forearm to guide her back to the warm ranch kitchen.

Page looked at Quaid, hardened. "No, you're brother doesn't want me here."

"Let's talk it over. Woman to woman. C'mon."

Chagrined and shivering with the cold, Page acquiesced. The gals went back to the house while Quaid remained outdoors. Kaitlin threw a towel in the microwave and in a couple of minutes wrapped it around Page's cold feet. She poured them coffee, afterwards cracking some eggs in a pan and putting bread in the toaster. As they sat eating their breakfast, Page related her stupidity at going up into the mountains unprepared and almost going over the edge. At the same time, she steered clear of any personal revelations.

Quaid returned around lunchtime and finished off the beans and B-B-Q the gals had left.

"So can you spare me, little brother?" Kaitlin asked while he ate. "Earth to Quaid, Earth to—" She waved her hand in front of his face.

Quaid snapped out of his reverie. "Huh?"

"I said, I'll take Page back home long enough to pack her clothes and then bring her back by dinner. If you can spare me."

"Might as well stay there. She doesn't seem to like it here very much," he muttered, chewing on a toothpick.

Worried and missing the cat immensely, Page said, "It's just that Sam's been alone all this time."

"Sam, where is your precious Sam? Figured you'd call him first thing this morning. Ought to be on his way. If you meant anything to him, he'd be here. The road's clear."

"Quaid!" Kaitlin chided. Turning to look at Page, she said, "I guess we were so busy getting acquainted I forgot to ask, just who and where is Sam?"

Before Page could answer, Quaid hissed, "Just get her out of here," as he threw a jacket over his shoulder and shoved the screen door open with the palm of his hand.

CHAPTER FOUR

Quaid stood currying his prize gelding. He didn't mean to brush so hard nor was he aware he was doing so until the horse stomped and sidestepped to get away.

"What was I thinking bringing a strange woman to the ranch?" he said to the buckskin. "I'm a damn fool. Thought she was single. Alone. Helpless. Serves me right. Why ain't she wearin' a weddin' band, Windrunner?" Aware of his annoyance, he wondered what bristled his dander. It wasn't as if they had any kind of relationship. She was just a stranded motorist that needed some temporary help. Was it because after eight years of being alone the loneliness was seeping into his bones?

"Wouldn't you know the first time I meet someone I could take a fancy to, she's married. No doubt loves this Sam character. Well, why shouldn't she? Suppose that's only right."

Windrunner nickered.

He'd let his defenses slip, that's what it was, finding himself more than mildly interested in her. He couldn't allow that. A woman would take advantage of you every time if you let them.

Denise had burned him good. That was eight years ago, but it might as well have been yesterday. He had fallen for Denise's charms thinking they shared the same goal: ranching. But she had been a fake. She had played along with him making him think his dream of being a cattle rancher was her dream too. When he had saved a good sum of money to put down on some land, he'd bought them an Airstream trailer to live in until they could build a house. Denise balked. He conceded to living in an apartment in town for a spell, but apartment rent and Denise's reckless spending took needed cash away from building the ranch.

Denise refused to get her hands dirty; most of the time she stayed in town forcing him to work alone. For every step forward, it seemed a half a dozen were backwards. As she demanded more and more of his time and attention, complaining of being alone too much, the strain and stress in their marriage grew. The more he tried to enjoin her help, the more she drew away. The night he returned home after a hard day of putting up fence only to find Denise had taken the neighbor to bed was the day he packed out.

He had worried she might try to take a share of the land he had struggled to obtain, but apparently she had no interest in him or the land. However, the cash settlement in the divorce put him into bankruptcy, and he'd had to work for other ranchers, drawing pay, in order to hold on to his little acreage. Meanwhile, Denise left town like tumbling tumbleweed.

Determined it would not happen again, he didn't place women high on his list of priorities. Not that he didn't look. He was still human. But he'd determined never to get close to a woman again, no matter how attractive or intriguing one might be. Which Page Chandling was. Kait's sweater and jeans had embellished her womanly curves. Bustier than Kait, the drawn material across her chest had accentuated her full bosoms. But seeing her long thighs and cleavage this morning weakened him in the knees.

He didn't realize how much he'd missed female companionship. Just having someone to talk to over coffee had brought back a warm, fuzzy feeling. Watching her snuggle into his robe, he couldn't help but wonder what it would be like to snuggle up with her in bed. Then, when their legs had accidentally bumped each other's under the table . . . whoo! it was like being zapped with a cattle prod.

"Good riddance, Page Chandling. Nuthin' but trouble."

Windrunner bobbed his head as if in agreement, then shook

However, Quaid couldn't shake the view of her standing there in his kitchen, yawning, his shirt rising to show her panties. Her hair tousled from the night's sleep. Like hell he wasn't looking. A man could look but not touch, couldn't he? He'd seen hotties at the bar in town but he would never date one. Bar flies were a dime a dozen. He knew what he wanted in a woman. She would have to stand beside him in good times and bad; help on the ranch and share his dreams; a woman not afraid of hard work, of getting her hands dirty, calloused and sore; a woman that would worry about a breech calf as much as a kid in bed with a fever; someone who knew the value of a dollar; and someone willing to warm his sheets on a cold Wyoming night. But was there such a person?

"Nice horses," Page commented as she walked into the barn, the steam from her breath billowing in the chill air. The coat, boots, hat and gloves Kaitlin had provided her felt cozy and warm against the freezing, buffeting wind. The gray sky and snow-covered earth shed little light in the stable. Steam rose from the horses' nostrils, mixing with the smell of hay, urine and excrement, as she stood near the stall where Quaid was brushing a gelding.

"I told Kaitlin she didn't need to take me home. I can drive back to the motel myself. I'll be leaving now." She hoped he had gotten over his irritation; it would be nice to have these two as her first friends in the new life she was determined to build here in Wyoming. Kaitlin seemed pleasant enough, but her brother could sure use some improvement.

Without looking up from grooming the horse, he gave her a curt, "Bye."
Is he that anxious to be rid of me?

"I want to thank you for all you did for me." Admiring the horses, she walked up to the gelding he'd been currying. She rubbed its nose, feeling its soft silkiness. "They look like fine racers." Hopefully that would get him talking.

Quaid stopped brushing the horse, wondering if he had heard right. "This here ain't a thoroughbred. You see those short legs?" He smoothed his hand over the gelding's flanks. "See how well muscled his flanks are? Look at this jaw line. Good stout neck. Good piece of horseflesh here. This here is a quarter horse, lady. Best ranch horse around. Great endurance. High speed for short distances. Good cattle cuttin' horse."

Ill at ease by her lack of horse knowledge, yet pleased he was speaking to her again, she said, "They all look pretty much the same to me, except for colors and those big Budweiser beer horses." She watched him as he patted the gelding's flank.

He shook his head. *She's pathetic.* "Those 'beer horses' are Clydesdales. Draft horses. Not worth a lick around cattle. . . I thought I told you to pack out." He shut the gate and moved to the next stall.

His words stung. Standing there, Quaid's words sliced through her making her feel worthless as compost.

Someone with more spunk would have set him straight then and there, but it was obvious she was out of her element. The rawness of her life with Michael still influenced her and though she wanted to assert herself, it was just too difficult for her. She feared the possible repercussions. Confrontations were too traumatic, but damn it, how was she ever going to change if she kept remembering Michael's manipulation and control? Sighing, she turned back toward the house.

"I wondered where you went to," Kait said, meeting her halfway. "I'm ready to go whenever you are."

After a slight altercation about driving her back to the motel, Page reluctantly gave in.

*   *   *   *

Page arrived at the Wagon Wheel to find a half starved kitty. "Sammy! You poor thing," she cried as she opened the door and Sam came running to her. Starved for attention, he meowed while weaving between her legs. She quickly opened a can of cat food, gave him fresh water, and then cleaned out the overused litter pan. While Sam ate, she changed out of Kaitlin's clothes. Handing the bundle to Kaitlin she said, "Thanks for the clothes. I'll be all right now. Thank your brother for me too; he doesn't seem to want to talk to me."

Kaitlin smiled while ignoring the gratitude. "Sam is your cat? Did you tell Quaid that?" She bent down to stroke the yellow feline. Sam returned the affection with loud purrs.

"I never got the chance," Page said lamely. "He went stalking off to the barn and when I went out there we . . . well, it just never came up. . . the timing wasn't right or something. But it's clear to me your brother wants nothing to do with me."

41

Rising, Kait said, "That brother of mine . . . he can be so obstinate and rude sometimes. Just wait until he finds out Sam is a cat. I can't wait to see the look on his face. And Sammy boy, you'll love it out in the barn." She grabbed him up in her arms, scratching behind his ears.

Page was confused. Kait talked as if she were returning to the ranch. Hadn't Kait been listening to her?

She dawdled while Kaitlin rattled off some necessities for a Wyoming winter. "Boots, heavy socks, long-legged underwear if you have any, heavy coat. . ."

Page planted herself squarely in front of her. "I'm not going back, Kait."

"Oh, I think you better. Quaid will have my head if I don't bring you back. You need someone to look after you for a few days and despite my brother's deplorable attitude, I think he's taken a shine to you."

Page opened her mouth agape, batting her eyelids open and close, murmuring, ". . . could've fooled me," although her heart fluttered at the prospect. He certainly hadn't given her a clue he was interested, so what made Kaitlin say such a thing?

"C'mon, once he sees that Sam is a cat he'll come 'round. And if you're uncomfortable at the ranch alone with him, I can stay overnight for a day or two."

Strangely, the motel room immediately seemed claustrophobic after being at the ranch. The openness of the range, the ranch house, the stables, even Chester and Blue seem to be beckoning. She started gathering her belongings, silent and in deep contemplation, vacillating while Kaitlin entertained Sammy. The chance at struggling with the land and its elements was partly what had drawn her to the West. Dreams of roaming mountains and plains like the mountain men, subsisting on game and fish, surviving by her wits. Cowboys and Indians and horses and hard work had also filtered through her dreams. Maybe ranch life would be just as exciting and challenging as a mountain man's survival. There were probably plenty of hardships and toughening up skills on a ranch. It might even serve as an apprenticeship preparing her for the harsher life in the wilds.

One minute she was thinking of becoming a self-sufficient woman of the wilds, the next she felt inexplicably drawn to the ranch. Although adamant she wasn't ready for a relationship, she couldn't help feeling strangely drawn to the enigmatic Quaid Kincaid. In spite of being nothing like the rough, tough, gun totin' carousing heroes of her novels, he did have that rugged cowboy persona, all muscle and sinew. But he didn't wear spurs or a gun belt. He didn't smell of whisky and she'd never seen him roll a cigarette, so she assumed he didn't smoke. Even though he cursed, she'd never seen him chew or spit. He didn't address her as ma'am anymore, which she rather missed. So dour and curt, she wondered how he impressed others. Maybe it was a cowboy thing. Sensitive to a fault, his personality left a lot to be desired.

Although she'd only been in Wyoming a few days, she was already disappointed there were no gun-totin' cowboys at the ranch, no wild Indians in the hills, no drunken cowhands in the bunkhouse, in fact, very little semblance to her novel reading. Was she just a big dreamer? Didn't any of those things exist? Her thoughts turned to the chocolate eyed cowboy wondering what his life entailed. Maybe that explained Quaid. Maybe he *was* a rough, tough cowboy. Maybe he went to the bar on Friday nights and got into fights. Maybe ...

What am I doing even thinking of him? He obviously has no use for me, in spite of what his sister says.

Yet her mind kept returning to the ranch. Unfamiliar with ranch equipment, in the few short hours she had been there, she had paid little heed to the machinery and tools, the wire, the lassos, tack and other accoutrements necessary to run the ranch efficiently.

43

Rather, she enjoyed seeing the horses in the barn and wished she could go out to the pasture to see the cattle and pet them. She liked spending time with Kait too whose friendliness made her feel welcomed. *But Quaid? He thinks Sam is a husband or boyfriend. Could he be jealous? No, not unless . . . unless. . . Get a grip, Chandling. I don't even like the man.*

Although Kaitlin was urging her to return to the ranch, she wasn't sure she could endure more of Quaid's aloofness. Stopping in her tracks, she stopped vacillating, deciding if she was going to become tough and self-sufficient she must refuse the offer. She had to stop being a wuss. Besides, she was feeling better by the hour.

"I told you I could have driven here myself. Now I have to find a way to get my car back. Besides, your brother doesn't want me there, even if he does find out Sam is my cat," she argued.

"Look, Quaid hasn't been around women for a long while. Maybe his skills are rusty. But my understanding is you need someone around in case the carbon monoxide has side effects. It's only for a couple of days. Dr. Dunacker can check you out after that and if you're okay then you can return here."

Not one to hold her ground well in arguments and at a disadvantage without her car, what choice did she have but to give in? She would have to pay her way of course. Could she afford it? What would they expect? Quaid alluded she should become familiar with the ranch. Would she have to work for her keep? She didn't know anything about ranching. What if Sam ran away? Or the dogs got him?

She glanced at the calendar with the curled pages on the wall. Ten days! She'd been in Wyoming ten days already. Two of them in the hospital. She shuddered to think of her bills. Between the motel and the hospital, she'd be out on the street if she didn't find a job soon. Add on room and board at the Kincaid's and. . . .

"I'd like to, Kait, but I can't afford to."

"Who said anything about money?"

"I can't stay free gratis. It just wouldn't be right. Now that I've got this hospital bill hanging over my head, I just don't know. I'm finding out Wyoming is expensive. I'm not sure I brought enough money with me. Even staying here in the motel is more expensive than I ever thought it would be."

"Then it's settled. You'll come back with me to the ranch. And if you feel guilty we'll find something for you to do."

Resolved she wasn't going to win the argument and hoping it would only be for a few days, Page reluctantly agreed to go back. However, she set her mind, telling herself that this time she was ready for anything, even Quaid Kincaid.

CHAPTER FIVE

Motel? The jerk couldn't even provide her with a home? This Sam must be a real loser.

Fighting with his thoughts since the girls left earlier, and feeling used, Quaid wished he'd called some of the phone numbers written on scraps of paper stuck in her wallet. He'd had plenty of time to search through her purse while she lay in the hospital. All he'd bothered with was identification. Maybe there had been a picture of this Sam character. Sam could have come to the hospital. Should have. Why hadn't he? Maybe he didn't care for her. If that were true why would she travel with him? Perversely, why was he even curious?

Never being a snoopy type, he was forthright and respectful, expecting his relationships to be the same way. Male or female. He expected Page to be loquacious, to tell him anything he needed to know. However, she was either timid or guarded. Was she hiding something? She appeared to chat easily with Kaitlin. Maybe she just couldn't communicate with men. Then again, why care? If she was married, she belonged with her husband. Filled now with regret, he should have left it to the hospital to hunt down next of kin.

He saddled up the gelding. *Imagine her thinking all horses are the same. He snorted, amused. Clydesdales! Geez, didn't she ever read a book? Watch TV?*

Glad she was gone and his responsibilities over, he took Windrunner for a short ride. He needed time alone; time to redirect his focus on his goal. Time to forget Page Chandling. He led the gelding out of the stall into the yard, swung up into the saddle and took off at a walk. As he reached the southwest pasture, the ground was wet and soggy, the warm sunshine melting the snow at an incredibly fast rate. He gave the gelding his head and they galloped off, mud splattering its flanks.

The lavender shadows of evening streaked the sky when Quaid came in for dinner. As he set foot in the mudroom it struck him that things were not right. Coats and jackets were on hooks. All the boots and galoshes sat in a row rather than their usual haphazard arrangement. He swiped the sweat from his forehead with his sleeve, before hanging his hat in a wire hat holder on the wall and going into the kitchen. The kitchen table was clean of all invoices, mail, receipts, equine catalogs and stacked papers. Peering around the corner all the *Western Horseman* magazines were stacked neatly in a pile under the sofa table. The living room tabletops were clean and void of everything but a couple pens, a scratch pad and a coaster. There wasn't a dirty glass or mug in sight. Everything was neat and orderly. *Now why would Kait mess up my system? She's never gone out of her way to clean house before. He went over to the stove and lifted a lid. UMMM, pot roast.* Under another lid were potatoes. Kait was really outdoing herself.

"Hi, bro. Dinner's almost ready. We've just about finished with the bedroom." Kait and Page walked into the kitchen with satisfied accomplishment on their faces.

"Finished what?" He turned to look at her. Seeing Page again, he bristled, dropping the pot lid on the stove making it clang before falling to the floor.

"Cleaning, of course. Your dust bunnies must be seven years old."

"Guess it's not a priority with me," he mumbled, stooping to pick up the lid. He was about to replace it on the pot when Kaitlin grabbed it out of his hand and went over to the sink to rinse it off.

Before he had a chance to open his mouth, Kait interjected, "Listen up, brother, Page has something to tell you."

Page approached him holding a soft cloth carrier. "Meow, Meow."

"What the—"

"Quaid Kincaid, I'd like you to meet Sam, the only man in my life." She unzipped the bag, and lifted Sam out, dangling him in Quaid's face. Gradually, the girls could not contain themselves; the sheepish look on his face set them giggling.

"Ooh better look out, brother. Looks like you got real competition there," Kait razzed as she smacked him with a twisted dishtowel.

"Huh. Guess you got me on that one." Knowing he'd been had, he said nothing more and went to the sink in the mudroom to wash up. *A cat. She was worried about a damn cat. I guess that means she's single. At least I won't have to worry about some irate husband beating the shit outta me.* As Kait and Page set the table, he sorted through the mail, afterwards commenting on the clean surroundings.

"Don't look at me. It's all Page's doing. She's even teaching me a thing or two about cooking. I think she's trying to 'earn her keep'." Kait turned to wink at her brother as he came up behind her.

He looked at Page. "Now why didn't I know that?"

Turning back to Kait, he said, "Well, it looks nice but it puts a crimp in my system; I won't be able to find anything now."

"And what system would that be?" she asked.

He threw his hands up in exasperation. "I don't suppose you know where my vaccine order is? It was right here on the table." Who did Page Chandling think she was to come in and turn his home topsy-turvy?

Page put Sam on the floor and went over to an old, scarred roll-top desk in the corner. Reaching into one of the cubbyholes, she pulled out a stack of rubber-banded papers. "These are orders and invoices. Utility bills are in that other cubbyhole and your correspondence is on the shelf. All your magazines and catalogs—"

He stood with his hands on his hips, impatient. "I know where they are. I saw them. You've been a little busy-body this afternoon, haven't you?" He peered over the neatly arranged contents.

Kait walked over to him and punched him in the arm. "Be nice."

"I'm always nice," he said in a flat monotone.

Page wondered if he was purposely antagonizing her or if he was always so ornery. Why couldn't he be grateful? She had simplified his life, so what was eating him now? Were all cowboys like this? Before she knew it, she blurted, "Well, excuse me. Kait and I worked all afternoon to clean up this pigsty. If that's all the gratitude you have you deserve to live like a pig. I didn't want to come back here. Kait talked me into it. But you are so rude, so ungrateful. . . so . . . " She couldn't find the words she wanted, so added, "Ugh!" Ducking under the table, she looked for Sam who had fled her arms. He cowered near a table leg. She grabbed him, holding him tight as he wiggled against her restraint. Standing, she announced, "I *want* to go home."

"I told you she didn't want to be here," Quaid said to Kaitlin.

Ignoring the remark, Kait said, "Let's just get through dinner peaceably. Page, you can help me put the food on the table." She handed Page bowls of potatoes and biscuits.

To appease Kait, Page temporarily resolved herself to his arrogant demeanor, praying under her breath that her time around him would be short. Her life had been traumatic enough with Michael. She didn't need a repeat performance.

Page set Sammy down and grabbed the bowls from Kait's hands. She sat down resentful at having to eat with His Highness. Ready to dig in, she became aware of the quietness as both brother and sister had their heads bowed. It had been ages since she'd heard grace, but she bowed her head along with them.

"Do you always say grace?" she asked after the amen.

"Don't you?" Kait asked.

Page shook her head. Religion hadn't played a big part in her marriage to Michael.

"Out here we thank the Lord for everything. If you stay out here long enough, you'll understand why," Quaid said.

"What does that mean?"

"Not many folks can stand the life, the land, the weather for long. They wimp out. Average newcomer only stays four, five years."

As she spooned potatoes on her plate, it surprised her to hear Quaid revert the conversation back to their cleaning.

"Hold on there. I'm just saying I'm not use to having someone tidy up after me. Give me time. I might get used to it."

Kait smiled. Leaning over she whispered in Page's ear, "He's trying."

Quaid leaned back in the chrome and vinyl dinette chair waiting for dessert. He studied Page. What was she doing back here when she so obviously couldn't stand it? Apparently, the carbon monoxide had left her system. Her cheeks had a nice rosy glow. She had pulled her blonde hair back with some clip thing he didn't care for and on the rare occasions she smiled, as she was doing now, her teeth were orthodontic straight and exceptionally white. She looked well with the exception of her blue eyes. They appeared dull and empty. Why? What could have possibly happened to this beautiful woman to make her look so sad?

He forked another piece of apple pie in his mouth as he studied her clothing. "That's some get up you got on."

Oh no, not another Michael. "And what's wrong with what I'm wearing?"

He had to admit she looked hot in her mid-thigh, black leather skirt with knee-high black leather boots but it was as far from ranch wear as one could get.

"Nothing, if you're in Chicago, I reckon. Hope you got some other clothes with ya though." He hung his head, shoveling another forkful in his mouth, so she couldn't see the amusement on his face. "Be hell muckin' stalls, or fixin' fence in that getup."

Kait wondered why her brother was being so rude. He no longer had reason to be jealous. Normally he was pleasant and easy going. What was it about Page Chandling that rubbed him the wrong way? Could he in fact be attracted to her? Or had he just lived alone too long?

Kaitlin observed Page sitting demurely at the table not offering much in the way of conversation. A twinge of envy rose as she admired how Page's blond hair fell into place flawlessly; it made her conscious of her own brunette locks that frizzed at the ends and seemed to have a mind of their own. Page's clothing and demeanor smelled of money. Looking at the black leather skirt and knee high boots, the flawless makeup, the well-manicured hands, she felt rather shabby in worn jeans from the TSC store, her Wellington work boots scratched and caked with mud, her jagged edged fingernails with the torn cuticles of work worn hands.

She found it strange this woman would come out to Wyoming all by herself. Most transplants were men or families. Wyoming was a rugged land that took a tough hide both internally and externally. Natives were so accustomed to the hardships they took it in stride. However, Page didn't appear to have the tenacity needed to survive the West; she seemed too fragile. So why would this classy, city girl purposely choose such a tough lifestyle?

The noise of pots and pans, water running, and the smell of coffee brewing woke Page the next day. She clawed in the dark for the alarm clock, turned it towards her and read its illuminated face: 4:30 a.m. Groaning, she sunk back on the pillow. Not again. Was this a daily routine?

There was a knock followed by Kait's voice. "Rise and shine. Coffee's on. You can help me muck out stables today. Later we'll run into town and get vaccine at the feed store. By the time we get back it should be lunchtime."

Page dressed quickly in her Versace jeans and a cashmere sweater in the drafty room and went to the kitchen. First light was breaking as she poured herself a cup of coffee. Looking out the kitchen window her breath caught. She whispered, "Look! Deer!" The large eared deer pawed at the new fallen snow searching for a morsel of food. Watching wildlife always made her feel peaceful, protective, nurturing.

She quietly went through the mudroom, cautiously opening the door a crack to gain a closer view. Her eyes lit on the outside thermometer. Twenty below. How wicked. It never got that cold in Leitchfield. A mean biting wind made her shiver, forcing her to shut the door quickly and quietly, but not before whispering to Kait, "C'mere. Look out there. I've never seen a deer like that." She pointed out past the barn.

Kaitlin opted to look out the small kitchen window. "Those are pronghorns. They're antelope. Extremely fast. They make wonderful steaks."

Page turned up her nose, curling her lip at the distastefulness of killing and eating such a beautiful animal. She continued watching it hop like a rabbit before breaking out into a fast run, only half listening as Kait tried to explain the difference between white tailed deer, mule deer and the pronghorn. "They're so beautiful," Page said, awestruck.

"What's beautiful?" Quaid asked, rounding the corner to the kitchen.

"The deer, the pronghorns," Page said, glancing out the door only to find them gone. "You just missed them."

"Hmm, I guess," he grunted. "They make good eatin' though." He poured himself a cup of joe, making a face as the scalding liquid went down his throat. He grabbed one of the bear claws Kaitlin had brought back with her when the gals returned from town. Eggs fried in a pan and the sound of bacon sizzled in the broiler. It was good to have women in the kitchen.

After a hasty breakfast, Quaid excused himself, snatching another bear claw for the road. In between bites, he put his snowsuit on, boots, a ski mask and the snowsuit hood. "Days wastin', now wheres my gloves?" he called into the kitchen as he felt through his pockets. Not finding them, he felt through his other jackets.

"They should be on that top shelf," Page volunteered.

He rolled his eyes. "What the hell they doin' up there? Don't make no sense. Always keep 'em in my pockets," he muttered. "Thanks," he spat as he pulled them off the shelf. He came back into the kitchen, poured another coffee and put a sip top over the mug before walking outdoors. The cold almost took his breath away. His eyes teared as he alternately crooked the coffee mug close to his body while putting on his gloves.

"Better eat hearty. You're going to work up an appetite," Kaitlin said, noticing Page had only eaten two strips of bacon.

Page accustomed to having Michael tell her what she could eat so as to keep her figure, rarely indulged in anything as decadent as sweet rolls. Yet they were a weakness for her and it didn't take much urging from Kaitlin before she was munching down a bear claw before rising to bundle up before going to work.

"Brr, is it always this cold?" Page asked, running after Kaitlin, who was on her way to the barn. As she caught up with her she added, "Thanks for letting me wear your snowsuit and stuff. I don't have anything warm enough for this kind of weather."

"You're welcome."

Page giggled as she watched Kait waddle in Quaid's oversized clothes. When Kait turned to look at her questioningly, she said, "Sorry, you look a little like the Michelin man."

"Thanks a lot," Kait chuckled, taking a handful of snow off the door handle and tossing it at Page.

Page laughed. It felt good to be lighthearted and playful. Did she know Kaitlin well enough to return the snowball or should she let it pass? She found herself wishing it had been Quaid. *If he'd just lighten up. Smile. He'd be so much nicer to be around if he'd laugh, have fun.*

Page moaned. "How can you stand this? My face is freezing. Back east, we'd be hunkered down in our homes." Page put her hands up to her stinging face.

"That's what city folk do. Chores don't stop out here. Just makes us work a little faster to get things done. Pull that ski mask down over your face or you'll freeze your brains. . . This weather keeps up we're going to have to feed the cattle. They won't be able to find any grass under all this snow. This cold, we may even find a yearling frozen."

Page winced at the thought of an animal freezing to death.

A moment later Kaitlin said, "Shovel shit, shovel hay, take your pick. Either way it will warm you up if you're working." Steam rose from her breath as she faced Page with a shovel and a hay rake.

Page hoped mucking stables didn't take long. It was so cold she couldn't feel her face. Her nose prickled as if acupunctured and she was sure her watery eyes would freeze shut. She pulled the ski mask over her face. It cut the cold, but did little to relieve her stinging eyes and nose.

"Speaking of work, I need to get a job. Sooner the better," Page said, wrinkling her nose at the smell as she shoveled manure into a cart. "I studied interior design once."

"Not much call for architects or interior designers around here. Not much new construction goes on. Maybe in Cheyenne or Cody. You might find a secretarial position at the mines or the drilling company though. Those are your two best bets. Not a whole lot of jobs here. We kind of live with bare essentials: plumbers, lawyers, feed stores. Know anything about land management? Water rights?"

Page shook her head at the alien terminology.

"Real estate? Waitressing?"

"No." However, after catering to Michael, waitressing couldn't be all that difficult. Still her preference

55

would be working in an office. Recalling the chiding Quaid gave her for cleaning, maybe she should look for a job as a maid.

As she shoveled, her thoughts danced back and forth, between her future and her past. Jobs were plentiful back in Leitchfield even though Michael refused to let her work. Finding employment in the West sounded like it would be more challenging.

The cold bit into her jaw, the one Michael had broken. It had happened just after he served her with the divorce papers. Countersuing had made him mad. He'd stormed in one night with a loaded shotgun. In the midst of arguing, rather than shoot her, he'd used the butt end to crack her in the face. Later, seeing what he had done, he apologized profusely and even withdrew the divorce papers.

However, that had been the final straw for Page; using the rehab time to gain the strength to leave him, she filed against him. Now, the cold weather making her jaw ache was a reminder of his abuse. And although she'd healed physically, the mental scars were still there.

Dust motes and chaff floated through the air making her nose itch as the sun rose over the horizon, filtering through the barn windows. She sneezed. Setting down the shovel, she walked to the barn door, opened it a crack and admired the beauty of the coming day.

"Page?"

"Huh?" She snapped out of her reverie.

"Anything wrong?" Kait paused, the hay rake in mid-air. "Gimme a hand with the water buckets."

"Sorry. Caught me daydreaming."

For one more moment, she stared out the barn doors at the rising sun shimmering on the snow tipped mountains in the distance. Mountains always held her captive. She stood mesmerized, connected to them in some strange way. Was that what it meant when someone spoke about his or her spiritual place? She wondered if this could be hers. Uncertain she had done the right thing in coming to Wyoming, yet drawn by some unknown force, just like the one she was feeling at this moment, she turned back to help Kait, questioning what it all meant.

CHAPTER SIX

Quaid returned around lunchtime to an empty house with nothing on the stove. Opening the refrigerator door, he peered inside then promptly shut it. He looked in the cupboards. "Beans! I wish the girls were here. They'd probably have something good fixed." Grumbling to himself, he poured a cup of coffee from the electric pot that was replenished and plugged in all day. He wondered how long it would be before the girls returned from town, which reminded him, he'd left Kait and Page in charge of chores this morning. He wondered what 'Miss Priss' did while Kait worked.

He was grateful Kait was there to play nursemaid as he wasn't about to teach a greenhorn the rudimentary elements of ranch life, no matter how attractive Page Chandling was. And she was a knockout now that the carbon monoxide had left her system. Her blue eyes shone like a fine blue crystal. Her cyanotic lips had turned pink and full and when she ran her tongue over them, he found it sexy and erotic. Reticent around him, she was bubbly like Doris Day around Kaitlin. Why the difference, he puzzled. He smiled recalling her excitement about the deer and antelope. Locals barely paid them any heed. She obviously liked animals. To see and hear her wonderment had been refreshing. The sound of feminine voices coming through the door interrupted his thoughts.

"Hey, you're home early," Kait said, setting down a couple sacks of groceries. "Have you eaten yet?"

"Naw, I was kinda waitin' on you. 'sides, nothin' here 'cept beans. What's in the bag?" He walked over to where Page was taking items out of a sack. He peered inside one and started pawing through it until she whisked the bag away.

"I thought I'd rustle up some chili and I got a cherry pie. Gonna take a few minutes though," Kait said, already removing the butcher paper from the frozen ground beef. She placed it on a plate, set it inside the microwave, and turned the dial to automatic defrost. She slid the pie out of the carton and sliced it into sixths.

Page asked, "What can I do?"

"Chop up some onions, open a can of tomatoes . . . a can of beans. Or shred some cheese."

"Chores get done this mornin'?" Quaid asked. He noticed Page was no longer in the fancy jeans and sweater she'd worn at breakfast. She had on black Levis that curved around her butt cheeks and outlined her legs. Her boobs looked soft and tantalizing under a robin's egg blue turtleneck. She was wearing Kaitlin's hiking boots. Her hair was loose again. He liked it better that way. It was sexier. He wished she wasn't so easy on the eye. Wyoming wasn't made for beautiful women. Wyoming was harsh; in time, wind and sun could ravage the most delicate of skin, turning it leathery and furrowed. Did she know that? *Why am I thinking like this? As soon as she gets a clean bill of health, she'll be out of my hair. Kait can return to Aladdin, and I can get back to normalcy.*

"Page is pretty handy with a shovel, bro. You should have seen her pitch into the manure this morning.

59

And she didn't plug her nose much at the smell," Kait said, as she opened a bag of chips and handed it to him.

"Yeah, but I did ruin my Versace's," Page added. "Here's that vaccine you wanted." She pulled a small sack out of the larger grocery bag and handed it to him.

Quaid didn't know what Versace's were, but he imagined she'd been devastated. Yet the tone of her voice didn't let on.

"Thanks," he grunted. *Well, I'll be . . . didn't think Miss Priss knew what work was.*

* * * *

Three days later, when Dr. Dunacker gave her a clean bill of health, she insisted on leaving the Double K. During her short time at the ranch, she found herself intensely drawn to Quaid, yet his demeanor left her cold. She offered to pay for her stay, but Quaid wouldn't hear of it. Nevertheless, she left fifty dollars on the kitchen table.

Once back in Newcastle, she plunged into finding an apartment and seeking employment. Over a week now in her one room apartment, she still had not heard from a single employer. After spending an entire week on foot, banging on doors, filling out applications, and hearing, "Don't call us, we'll call you," Kaitlin was right; work was scarce.

Page looked out the sole window of her little apartment where a lone mule deer grazed through scrub grass. Churning it up with its hooves, it didn't seem to find anything and meandered to a different spot. A favorite Bible passage, paraphrased, came to mind: "Consider the birds. . . God feedeth them. How much more does He care for you? Worry not." Its message always comforted her, although today, she couldn't feel God's goodness.

Rent, utility deposits, and gasoline had gobbled up her savings. Food prices were high and she was already tired of hamburger, hot dogs and beans. Jobless, in serious financial straits and lonely, it seemed things couldn't get much worse. Stories of Hugh Glass, Jeremiah Johnson and Jim Bridger filtered through her mind as they trudged through snow, ice, and freezing cold-water creeks shooting game, trapping furs, and fighting off Indians. She thought how hard it must have been on the early womenfolk who endured the hardships of traveling over the land in wagons, having babies with no doctor present, trying to eke out enough food from the hard packed earth to feed a family. Yet they never gave up. Tenacity. How she envied it. She questioned if she had it in her. It had been easy to dream while sitting in the luxury of her Leitchfield home, but now she was facing reality. Was she strong enough to stick it out?

Although her circumstances were different from the pioneers, she was finding it incredibly hard to stay optimistic. She realized her earlier thoughts about the frontier and existing like a mountain man had all been fantasy. She could no more be like them than Donald Trump could be a street person. The reality was that in many ways, Wyoming appeared about twenty years back in time, but certainly no longer the Wild West or Mountain Men Era. It was a barren, lonely land except for the towns—the smaller ones still had an old western flavor with their old storefronts. No high-rises, no modern architecture yet modern day conveniences were present.

Wyoming was not the last frontier and other than character actors at the tourist traps, there were no modern day Wild Bill Hickok's, no Martha Jane Cannery's; no gun slingers, no main streets of dirt, mud, and manure; no soiled doves hanging out of brothel windows; no mountain men trapping beaver. Even the Indians in the nearby reservations weren't hostile. How foolish she had been to think there might be remnants of the Old West left. Part of her was disappointed and saddened by the fact, the other was happy not to be living that way.

She looked down at her hands; her fingernails, once beautifully manicured, were ragged and chewed almost to the quick. Restless, she picked up a book. She tried to read but couldn't concentrate. Pacing the floor, she waited for an employer to call, all the while worrying about her dwindling funds. She went to the closet for the umpteenth time, pulled an envelope out of her suitcase, and proceeded to count her money. Today's tally was one hundred sixty-two dollars. Not enough to last a month. Her security hinged on always having substantial savings. Although tight with expenditures, her security was now threatened. What would she do if she ran out of money? She hadn't counted on it costing so much to live in the West.

Saving up for the trip had been difficult. Michael controlled their finances. Her only means of saving money was to write grocery checks for twenty dollars over the amount of the bill, squirreling the cash away in coat pockets where Michael would not find it. If Michael complained about the grocery bills being higher than usual, she pleaded inflation or cut back to the normal budget.

"Oh, quit feeling sorry for yourself. You wanted to be out here. You think the pioneers never had a worry? Buck up. Forge ahead. I'm trying, but if I have to eat any more hot dogs and beans, I'd rather starve. I'm not out in the cold. . . Things aren't so bad," she said aloud hoping to bolster her flagging bravado. Nevertheless, her lecture didn't still her anxious heart as her mind played a broken record: I've got to get a job or else. . .

Even Sam had deserted her for the wild allure of a barn and field mice. He refused to come out of his newfound hiding place before she left the ranch, so Page opted to leave him there hoping Quaid or Kaitlin would return him someday. However, she hadn't told either of them where she was living yet. She made a mental note to tell the Kincaid's her new address, while pondering if she would be there long enough or if circumstances would force her elsewhere. Maybe she'd call Kaitlin to let her know although it was really Quaid she wanted to tell. But, Quaid wouldn't care, would he?

The ringing phone jarred her thoughts back to the present. With hope strong in her heart that it would be an employment offer, she picked up the phone. Her brother's voice brought comfort and dread.

"Sis? What are you doing in Wyoming? Michael said you just took off deserting him. Somebody in your office said you wanted to see the West. So, are you just on a vacation, or what? Michael seemed concerned you hadn't called him. What's going on?"

Page closed her eyes. Of all the rotten luck. Someone had told Michael. Had she let her tongue slip while talking to the girls back in the office? *Deserted him? Deserted? What bullshit was Michael spreading now?*

"Sis? You there? I thought I'd come see ya for a couple of days. I have to go to Denver for a job interview and . . . Well, is it okay?"

Disguising the panic she felt knowing that Michael knew her whereabouts, she responded, "Okay? Is it okay? It's great! When will you be here? Day after tomorrow? Only two days? What job? How—"

As her brother disclosed his flight plans her thoughts wandered to Michael. *Who told him I'm in Wyoming? How dare he say I deserted him! Is he trying to find me? Should I stay? Go? What is he up to? At least if he shows up while Trevor is here, I'll have a witness.* She tuned back into what Trevor was saying.

"Slow down, I'll tell you about it when I arrive. I'll be in Denver about 2:20 Wednesday, or thereabouts."

"Umm, that's about six hours from here when the weather is good. You might have trouble finding me in the dark. This isn't like Los Angeles you know. How about I pick you up?"

"That's a long haul for you, isn't it?"

"People out here don't think anything of it. I can do it, big brother. I haven't got anything better to do," she ended on a glum note. A bit more cheerfully, she added, "It will be so nice to have some company. But Trev, don't expect too much. It's kind of different out here."

As she replaced the phone, her surroundings glared at her like a full moon. How embarrassing to have Trevor with a five-figure income see her little apartment. The Trevor she knew wasn't the type to lower himself to such humble digs. Where would he sleep? She only had a sofa bed. Moreover, how would she entertain and feed him on a hundred sixty-two dollars? With Trev coming, she wouldn't have time to look for a job either. Happy her brother was coming, she also felt doomed she'd be on the streets when he left.

The day before Trevor's arrival, the weather shifted. Although it was late October, a warm Chinook wind from Canada came down making it Indian summer-like. She was glad that most of the snow had melted; I-25S would be free sailing clear to the Denver airport.

The Chinook boggled her though; it could be 65 degrees in town, yet snowy, even blizzard-like in the high elevations. Mother Nature sure was strange.

Antsy, anticipating her brother's arrival, she kept busy making cake, pie, and brownies. She looked forward to catching up with Trev. It had been several years since she'd seen him and she wondered if he had changed.

As she stood stirring a cake mix, her mind drifted back to her stay at the Double K. She missed the daily routine of ranch life, the girl talk and laughter with Kait, the horses, the mountains. She even missed Quaid. Although he irritated her to no end, he held her spellbound by his personification of the cowboy legend.

Looking at the clock, she wondered what Quaid would be doing as she helped herself to a cup of coffee from the pot she now kept perpetually brewed. Cowboy coffee. Black. She started drinking it that way after being at the Kincaid's. She smiled recalling her faux pas. Handing coffee with cream and sugar to Quaid, he had taken the hot cup from her, grimacing. "I ain't into that latté stuff," he had said, before dumping it down the drain, and pouring himself a "real" cup of coffee.

Quaid Kincaid, she liked how the name rhymed. She pictured him in her mind, remembering his broad shoulders and narrow hips. Lanky, yet strong and sinewy. And those eyes—dark pools of chocolate, soft yet piercing. His voice—a little gravelly, a little clipped, a voice filled with a strong sense of who he was. A loner. So different from Michael who was vivacious, a charmer, a ladies man. Impeccable Michael with his jet-black hair, each strand in place, his chic Armani suits, manicured nails and polished shoes, whereas Quaid wore flannel shirts and Levis, his sandy brown hair casual and windblown when he didn't have "hat hair". Michael's skin was white while Quaid's gleamed copper. Michael reeked of cologne while Quaid smelled of sunshine, soap and water. Both sexy, both intriguing. Sexy. Intriguing. Charming. All traits she should be wary of. Traits she had a weakness for. Well acquainted with Michael's jealousy, possessiveness, and controlling, she speculated what Quaid was like. He had shown a jealous streak when he thought Sam was a boyfriend. Would he be possessive and controlling too? Inhospitable, Michael wouldn't think of taking in a stranger, unless it was in his favor. Yet Quaid appeared the exact opposite of Michael. This no nonsense cowboy had taken her in not knowing a thing about her. Envisioning the care and tenderness he lavished on his horses, she somehow couldn't envision this moody cowboy being tender and caring toward any woman, yet what was behind his cool façade?

65

What was it Kait had said—he hadn't been around women for quite awhile. Yes, she could see how his personality would turn women away. *He was reclusive. Maybe something nagged at him. Maybe he had some baggage in his life that followed him around like Michael followed her. Or was it something else? If he disliked women so much, why had he taken her in? Moreover, why did she find him attractive?* The more she thought about him, the more tempted she was to call him at the ranch.

She picked up the phone. Dialed. Waiting for it to ring, Michael's voice coursed through her brain calling her a man-chasing whore.

"I'm not a whore. I'm not. Get out of my head, Michael," she said, replacing the receiver. "It's okay for a woman to call a man nowadays." But what if Quaid didn't feel that way? What if he thought she was chasing him? "Damn it, Michael. I hate what you've done to me." Now that Michael had infiltrated her thoughts, she couldn't talk to Quaid, even if he did pick up the phone. Would she never be free of Michael's malicious verbal abuse?

CHAPTER SEVEN

"Hey, Sis, remember how I used to draw beards and moustaches on your picture book characters? Boy, did you get mad."

Page laughed recalling the memory. Her books were her treasures. Why Trev had to deface them she'd never know. "I remember that . . . I used to scream, Mommmmm, Trev's making faces in my books. "

"And then I'd catch hell for it."

"Serves you right. Gosh, I can't tell you how good it feels to laugh Trev, especially at 6:30 in the morning," she said as she put strips of bacon on the broiler pan. "It's a great way to start the day."

Michael never appreciated laughter, saying it was childish and he wouldn't tolerate it. Page felt he was wrong, yet it was one more part of herself she'd subdued under his dominance. Swiping at her tearing eyes she continued, "I haven't laughed like this since. . ." The phone interrupted their reminiscing.

Her heart caught in her throat. *Michael! Had he found her? Had Trev said something?* Cautiously, she picked up the phone. "Chandling's."

"Page? Quaid. You, uh, left one of your gloves here. I, uh, thought maybe I'd drop it off to you this mornin', if that's all right?"

A glove? She hadn't been aware of losing a glove. How insignificant. But if Quaid thought it important enough to make a special trip to town, she wasn't going to discourage him. Just the thought of seeing him again brightened her day.

"Sure, okay," she chirped, as both relief and a wave of delight coursed through her. "How did you get my number? Did Kaitlin give it to you?"

She could hear the amusement in his voice.

"Connections."

She wondered what or who the connections were. "My address—"

"I know where you live."

She frowned. If Quaid could find where she lived so easily, it would be a snap for Michael to find her. She started to say something, then noticed he'd already disconnected. Hanging up the phone, she went back to scrambling eggs, the anticipation of seeing him quickening her step, sending ripples of joy through her heart.

Page and Trev had just cleaned their plates when there was a knock on the door. Page bound up eagerly. She opened the door a crack to be sure it was Quaid. "Quaid! I didn't expect you so soon. How did you get here so fast?" She opened the door the full swing. "Come in. Come in and meet. . ."

It may have been six thirty in the morning, but the sight before her eyes was better than a biscuit oozing with honey. Her face lit up at the sight of him. She skimmed over his pearl-buttoned western shirt, clean jeans, and polished boots. Damn! He was even sexier all dressed up.

A fragrance of men's cologne wafted from him and she thought she'd melt there on the spot. How could she have missed him so much in such a short time? While she was happy as a bunny in a burrow, Quaid displayed his usual dour expression.

At that moment, Trevor peeked around the corner, rose from his chair and came out to where Page stood. "Hi, I'm Trevor Harrison." He extended his hand.

Quaid looked over at him without letting on his surprise. He nodded acknowledgement. Quaid handed her a forest green glove.

She stared at the glove; it wasn't even hers. It was Kait's. As she looked up, Quaid was halfway to his truck. What happened? He couldn't leave. Not yet. Compelled to rush after him, she bolted out the door in her bare feet, hollering back to Trev, "I'll explain later."

"Quaid, wait!" she hollered, running to his truck. She pounded on the glass. "Let me explain."

He rolled the window down a couple of inches. Setting his jaw and staring straight ahead, he drawled, "Well?"

"This isn't mine. It must be Kait's."

"And I thought Sam was the only man in your life," he spat between clenched teeth.

What? He may as well as smacked her in the face. He thought. . . She had to explain if he would listen.

"Trev is my brother; he's just visiting." She tugged at the tie belt of her silky robe that had a habit of loosening and parting, exposing her cleavage. Shivering as the frosty air danced under the thin, silk robe and the cold pavement rose through the soles of her feet, she hopped from one foot to the other.

He twisted his head to look directly into her face. "You really expect me to believe that? You must think I was born in the back forty," he hissed.

"Quaid, please, it's the truth." Instantly aware the belt had loosened, exposing her, she pulled the robe back together, holding it.

He glanced over at her. "Uh, huh. Look at yourself. Tell me you're not sleeping with the guy."

"I'm not. He is my brother. If you'd simmer down and come inside. . ."

He turned to look straight ahead. "Don't play me, woman." Then turning to look into her face, he asked, "All I want to know is do you love him?"

"What? Well, yes. I mean, no. I mean yes I do, but—"

"That's all I needed to know." He shifted his gaze straight-ahead, shifted the truck into gear, ready to stomp on the accelerator.

Page clung to the door handle. What did it matter if she let her words fly? She'd probably never see him again. "You're nothing but a stupid, jealous cowboy."

"Let go," he said through gritted teeth.

His voice couldn't have been more icy, his face more stoic. Hurt by his coldness, she let go and stepped back. Tears pooled in her eyes as she watched him lead foot the accelerator and speed off. Her feet tingling from the cold, her skin a mass of goose bumps, Page dashed back into the house.

"That was short lived," Trevor, who had been watching from the window, said.

"Yeah, well. . . " she answered in a disgruntled tone of voice. Why couldn't he at least come in and get acquainted with Trev? Apparently, he's rude to everyone. No wonder no women want him. What a hothead.

"You like that guy?" Trev asked, watching his sister's reaction.

"I don't know. Sometimes I think I do, but other times. . . " Or was it that he represented ranching, his living off the land, that appealed to her? Thrilled when he'd called, she now felt disturbed. She could not understand him. He was acting like a jealous schoolboy. *Jealous. Like Michael.* If another man so much as made polite conversation with her Michael became a ranting maniac. During counseling with her pastor, she learned that jealousy was often a sign of insecurity. As much as she tried to remind herself of that, when Michael was "in one of his moods", it was difficult to believe he was insecure. Was Quaid's storming away a sign of his insecurity?

*   *   *   *

Between Kaitlin laying into him about being an ass while Page was at the ranch and his own thoughts, maybe he had been a little rough on her. Since she'd left the ranch, Quaid found she popped into his mind at the most awkward times. Yet he wasn't about to admit that she lit something long gone out in him. He told himself it was just physical attraction. He'd been alone too long. He surely couldn't be missing her; he barely knew her. Besides, she hadn't been gone long enough. But his mind kept rewinding back to her sleepy 'Good Morning', her snickering when she put one over on him with Sam, her smiles around Kaitlin, her awe with the animals, her jumping in to help with what needed tending. No, it wasn't her; it was him. He was annoyed with himself for caring, for being so interested. Annoyed he couldn't forget her.

In addition, she'd left Sam behind. Why would she do that? Sam was obviously special to her. If she missed him why didn't she come back to the ranch to get him? Or did she expect him to bring Sam back to her? The cat had taken to barn and outdoor life like second nature. Blue and Chester loved to chase him, but the cat always found a hidey-hole. Maybe she didn't need Sam now that she had, what's-his-name. Was she that fickle and uncaring with all her relationships?

Eventually, he had called Kaitlin, to find out where Page lived on the premise of returning Sam. But if she had known where Page moved to she wasn't telling. What was the big secret? As a last resort, he contacted an old girlfriend at the post office who supplied him with Page's address. All it took was a call to the telephone company and he had her phone number.

Although he could count the dates he'd had on one hand with fingers left since Denise left, all of a sudden he had a renewed interest in dating. Would Page be willing to go out with a poor cowboy? Why did he even think that when she had just told him she loved Trevor? His scheme to take Kait's glove to her with the express idea of asking her out hadn't worked as he'd planned. And running out to the truck in that slinky nightie. Listening to her breathiness, watching her jiggling breasts as she hopped from one foot to the other, he'd exited just in time as the stirrings in his groin caused an uncomfortable erection. Brother, smother. Like hell, she'd wear that in front of her brother. No woman of his would ever get away with that.

By the time he pulled into the feed store lot his temper had defused itself into a simmer, and he found himself regretting his actions. Had he impulsively jumped to conclusions again?

"Hey, Quaid," the clerk greeted him. "What can I do for you?"

"You got my order ready?" he barked.

"Geez, Quaid, I said I'd have it ready after three."

"Damn it, Morrison, I'm here now." Impatient, he fumed. He removed his dress Stetson, beating it on the leg of his jeans as if it were dirty, and scratched his head with his other hand.

"Don't have to bite my head off." Morrison rummaged through shelves and bins.

"SSShit. I'm sorry. I'm just a little hot under the collar. Guess I haven't cooled off yet." Quaid wandered over to another counter to look at bovine supplements before heading towards the door.

"I've never seen you cantankerous 'cept when there's a woman involved," the clerk said, stacking part of his order on the counter. "Must be special for you to get all dressed up."

Staring out the door, preoccupied, Quaid answered, "Yeah, women. Can't live with 'em, can't live without 'em.

The clerk chuckled. "You can say that again."

* * * *

Quaid's cruel remarks still stung her ears and pierced her heart days after Trevor's leaving. Although embarrassed by her financial situation, she told Trev where she stood and while she expected nothing from him, he had given her a check for $500. It was enough to take the edge off her worry for a few days, yet she was disappointed a man with a five-figure income couldn't be a little more generous.

"Five hundred is five hundred. Better than nothing. Well, Sammy, I've got one more interview. I better get ready and head for the feed store. Wish me luck." Sam sat contentedly on the windowsill sunning himself. He squinted as if to reply. Happy that Kaitlin had brought him back to her, Page had missed her companion, feeling crazy talking aloud to the four walls.

She put her outerwear on, grabbed her purse and house keys, kissed the top of Sammy's head and left the apartment. With ten minutes leeway before her interview, Page strolled the uneven sidewalks of Main Street taking stock of the businesses—a grocery store, a bank, an insurance agent, a post office, a feed store and a bar. She particularly liked the old empty buildings, the ones with the false fronts like in Western movies. Peering into the dirty glass windows, some still had decorative tin ceilings or a big potbelly stove in the center of the room. She tried to imagine what the establishment's first business had been

73

before her own hankerings to run a used bookstore flitted through her mind.

When two more days passed silently with no job offers, Page admitted defeat. "I guess our big adventure is over, Sam. No one's going to hire me. Cowboys are an enigma. There are no mountain men. No desperadoes. I guess I am just a dreamer, a Wyoming dreamer."

In a flash her bravado crumpled. "Oh God, I don't want to go home, but where do we go?" she wailed. Desperation and failure swept over her as she sat cuddling the large tabby in her lap. "Looks like its Social Services for us or we'll have to live on the streets." Her worst fear realized, she cried while nuzzling and kissing Sam to assuage her panic. He began purring loudly. Resolved she had no choices, she swiped at the tears with her hands, and then set him down on the windowsill. She went to pull her duffle bags from the closet.

"I've got to get some boxes at the grocery store, Sammy. Maybe even one for you to sleep in. I'll be back soon." With heavy heart, she plodded to her car.

Page returned to hear the phone ringing in her apartment. Hope crested, replaced with fear. Could it be Michael? Should she answer it? She had churned over Trevor's conversation, always coming to the same conclusion: How could Michael possibly find her? Wyoming was too large to find someone randomly. Yet Quaid had found her easily enough. Rushing through the door, she dropped the boxes on the floor, grabbed up the phone and nearly wilted when she heard a familiar voice.

"Would you like to go to a rodeo?"

Elation quickly replaced fear. When Quaid sped off the other day, she was sure she would never hear from him again. Did she want to go? Her heart fairly sang. Apparently, Quaid wasn't mad at her after all.

Packing could wait.

*   *   *   *

Music played in the background amongst thunderous clapping, hooting and hollering. The dirt arena churned up by horses and cattle sent particles through the air making her sneeze. As they took their bleacher style seats, the announcer came over the PA system, "Let's give the White River Rodeo Queen another big round of applause."

"We haven't missed much. The events are just going to start," Quaid said laying a horse blanket down on the wooden seat.

Her eyes darted everywhere trying to take it all in. Cowboys wearing big flashy belt buckles stood around the arena near the chutes. The announcer seemed to be up in a theater style box. Horses danced in chutes. Snorting bulls pawed the ground. Men on horseback twirled lassos. There were even clowns.

Unexpectedly, the noise became raucous as a rider charged out of a chute rearing and flaying.

"He's going to ride that thing?" she hollered to make herself heard above the crowd.

"Yep. That's what's it all about. See that strap on his flanks? Essentially that strap combined with spurring is what makes the horse buck. After that it's up to the rider to stay on for eight seconds."

Before she could respond, a buzzer went off and the announcer said, "Let's give that cowboy a hand. That was Les Memory from Austin, Texas riding BeBop." The crowd went wild.

"I take it he won?" she asked. "It happened so fast."

"It's a fast sport alright. Here comes the next one." He pointed her attention back to the ring.

"Okay folks, chute number four. Jackson Farmer from Cheyenne, Wyoming on Ball Breaker. With a name like that you better be ready, son." The tumultuous roar from the crowd drowned out his voice.

Page covered her ears. "Is it always this noisy?" she shouted.

"Especially when it's one of our own."

The cowboy had given his official nod he was ready, and the gate flew open in the middle of the announcement. The bronc reared and twisted, left, right, up, down. Page watched the cowboy hold on, his hand in the rigging, his legs and spurs working the unbroken horse. The horse bucked; Jackson drew his knees closer to his chest, dragging spurs into the horse's shoulders. As the horse descended, the rider extended his legs readying himself for the next jump.

Again the buzzer sounded. "That was some ride folks. Let's see what the judges say. 96! Ninety-six points folks. That's almost a perfect ride." Whistles and stomping joined the hand clapping.

Page sat enthralled by all the events. Compared to the bronc riding and steer wrestling, calf roping and barrel racing events seemed tame to Page.

"Now folks I know you've all been waiting for the Bull Riding," the announcer said. More whistling and clapping rose in the arena. "It's coming right up."

A few minutes later, Page watched a rider get whip lashed and jerked about. She could not understand why anyone would put himself through that unless he was a masochist. All of a sudden, the rider hung upside down atop the monstrous Brahma bull.

"Uh-oh, he's hung up in the ropes," Quaid said.

The crowd grew deathly silent as the young rider's head bounced inches from the arena dirt and the flaying hooves of the bull. Page flinched and cowered, covering her eyes, yet held by some perverse curiosity she peeked between her splayed fingers. Just then, the rider's rope released sending him to the dirt as the rear legs of the black monster flailed and came down on the cowboy's ribs. The cowboy lay still. Immediately the rodeo clowns ran in waving red bandannas and arms in an effort to divert the cavorting bull. When the young cowboy didn't pick himself up, a couple of other rodeo riders ran out, and the next thing she knew the bull headed back to a corral, while an ambulance siren wailed in the background.

Page could almost imagine the crunch of bones as she buried her face in Quaid's shoulder. "Oh my God, why would anyone want to do that? He's got to be hurt. I can't look."

There was a pause in the program while the medics carted the hurt cowboy off on a stretcher. Page was sure the rodeo had ended on this sad note. She felt Quaid stand up, drawing her up with him. Looking around, she saw the entire crowd rise up, clapping, giving the rider a standing ovation. The medics barely left the arena before the next contestant slid into the dirt, just seconds after leaving the chute; as he struggled to rise, the bull twirled stomping on his leg, crumpling him to the ground.

"We got us some mean bulls tonight, folks," the loudspeaker blared.

Page tugged at Quaid's sleeve in consternation.

"It's okay. He'll cowboy up. See he's already up," Quaid crooned in her ear.

Page watched in amazement as the cowboy dusted off his hat, and limped back to the gate. "But that bull kicked him. I saw it. How could he not be hurt?" she said, turning to face him and swallowing hard.

He slid his hand down to cover hers. "Don't upset yourself. It's just a sport. These guys have grown up around livestock. Now, I'm not sayin' no one never gets hurt but a cowboy's got to be tough. He's gotta show them ol' bulls who's boss. He sure don't want to get beat by a piece of baloney. They're getting paid a good purse—er, money. Besides, the clowns head off a lot of trouble. That's what rodeo is all about."

She listened attentively, noting the enjoyment and intense interest on his face. This was Quaid's world. She had to bite her tongue to keep from commenting on how dangerous and stupid she found it. Men were so vain riding around on animals that could pulverize them. Each time a rider got hung up or kicked she cringed. Yet there was a strange fascination seeing if the cowboy could hang on for eight seconds. In her distress, she hadn't felt his hand slip over on to hers. Consciously aware of it now, a warm feeling effused her. This was the first affection he'd ever demonstrated. His hand was warm and sweaty, smooth yet calloused. It completely covered her small hand. She pretended not to notice for fear he would withdraw it.

"That's it folks. Stick around for a little High Stakes Poker," the announcer said.

The crowd rose, milling towards the exits. A few men headed for the arena. *How strange.* "You mean they're going to stay and play cards?"

"Ever seen High Stakes Poker?" Quaid asked her as they stood and shuffled down through the bleacher seats with the crowd.

"Uh-un," she shook her head. "How can everyone here get in the game?"

"It's like this: Four cowboys sit at a card table out in the arena playing cards. Then they let a bull loose. The guys stick around and see if that bull can take 'em out of their chair. It can be a real hoot."

She rolled her eyes. *The games men play.*

"Let's watch a hand or two, and afterwards we'll go get a burger."

Page watched Quaid pull into a curbside slot at the Whitehorse Café. She watched a high school girl come out to the truck, order pad in hand. It made her think back to pictures she'd seen dating back to the 1950's of young girl's on roller skates bringing orders out to cars, but she could not remember ever going to one. Was the Whitehorse a relic of times past?

"Buffalo burger?" Quaid asked, turning off the engine.

"Buffalo?" she said strangely, turning up her nose.

"Beats hamburger any day."

"What's it . . . taste like?"

"Not much difference. A little drier. Most people try 'em prefer it over beef. Leaner. Not much fat. Try one?"

She gave a slight shrug of indifference before he leaned over to the speaker, ordering three burgers, two fries and two Cokes. When he turned his attention back to her she was smiling.

"What is it? What you grinning at?"

Amused, she said, "I've never been to a drive-in with car hops . . . I like it here."

CHAPTER EIGHT

Like two dumbstruck adolescents, they stood at the door to Page's apartment. Page dawdled wondering if Quaid would kiss her. She watched him as he looked at his boots, then back up at her. He'd start to say something, then drop it. She fidgeted in her purse for her keys, hesitated again wondering if he would kiss her. When it didn't happen, the awkwardness of the moment set in and Page put her key in the lock. Opening the door, she turned to face him. Should she invite him in? Not wanting him to see she had been packing, she said "goodnight", when she felt him take hold of her hand.

"Thanks for going out with me. Goodnight," he said, giving her hand a firm, quick shake before turning to walk back to his truck.

Had she been that bad a date? Or was this a cowboy thing? She'd never been on a date where the guy didn't at least attempt to kiss her.

Tonight had been fun, although she felt rusty as an old tin can in the dating department. However, seeing the lighter side of Quaid, she decided there might be hope for him yet. In fact, she would have to say she liked him, tonight. Quaid hadn't zinged her with any sharp barbs, and when he leaned over and spoke above the crowd in her ear, it sent little shivers through her. During dangerous moments in the arena, without thinking, she had buried her head in his shoulders and felt his strong arms fold around her, making her feel safe and protected. The buffalo burger was her first experience eating game and she decided she liked it. Tired, but happy, she undressed on her way to the bathroom. She washed a coating of arena dust off in the shower before going to bed with recollections of Quaid dancing through her head.

Was he supposed to kiss her? Not one to conform to rules, he wasn't comfortable with it. Besides, he didn't want to give her the wrong idea about their being together tonight. However, he'd felt like an awkward teenager on a first date. She'd looked a little surprised, maybe even disappointed when he shook her hand and thanked her for the evening. What was so wrong about that?

Driving home, he recalled the chiding Kaitlin had given him when he told her about the strange man sleeping with Page. Later, Kaitlin confirmed that indeed Trevor was Page's brother from Los Angeles and that he should stop acting like some silly jealous high school boy always jumping to conclusions. Swearing he'd have to be more trusting, he remembered how Denise had slept around behind his back. He knew he shouldn't put all women in the same category as her, but he couldn't help it. Since that time, finding trust was a difficult task. When he loved a woman, he gave his whole self over to her. And by god, he wasn't going to get hurt like that again.

Yet, he realized how reclusive he'd been, how he jumped at her about Sam, also about her brother, Trev. Impulsive, impetuous, jealous. If he were going to date again, he would have to take a chance. A chance with his heart. He just hoped she wouldn't tear apart what little Denise had left.

Being with Page tonight was like a breath of fresh air. Page's naiveté made the rodeo and the White Horse new and exciting again. He did his best to be polite, not come on too strong, but when she snuggled into his embrace, it left him wondering how far he should go. Had she been expecting more? He could still smell a whiff of her perfume. It smelled sweet as wild honeysuckle. She sure had a way of making him miss female companionship.

He flipped the radio on. "This is Baxter Black, signing off. . ." The radio announcer followed the closing with, "Say folks, if you all enjoyed hearing Baxter tonight, here's your chance to see him in person. Baxter Black is appearing at the Broken Cup Café in Sheridan, Wyoming one night only. That's October 25th at 7 p.m. Cowboy poet Baxter Black will be performing his all time classics along with some new material. This is a first come, first serve situation, so best get there early for a seat. Remember now, that's Baxter Black, The Cowboy Poet, at the Broken Cup Café in Sheridan, October 25th at 7 p.m."

Baxter Black was a favorite of Quaid's. He made a mental note to ask Page if she would like to go with him. The following evening he called her. "Would you care to go see Baxter Black with me a week from tomorrow? He's the best cowboy poet around."

"The 25th? I wish I could, but I'm afraid I have other plans."

Plans? How could she have plans? As far as he knew from the conversation the previous night, she still wasn't working, so that couldn't be it. *Another guy?* He tried to push the thought from his mind.

"Could you change your plans? He's only performing the one night."

"No, I'm sorry," she whispered, gently putting the phone back on the receiver.

Stymied, he wondered what he had done wrong. Recalling the previous night, he ran through a mental

checklist . . . no manure on the legs on his jeans . . . shaved
. . . wiped the mustard off his mouth at the café instead of
licking it off. Maybe he'd read the signs wrong. Maybe he
should have kissed her.

* * * *

Having to tell Quaid she couldn't see him again was
just too much. He'd called in the midst of her packing.
Overdue on her rent and scared the landlord would pound
on her door at any minute, she was already upset. Tears
rolled down her cheeks, the more she thought about
leaving, about not knowing where to go or what to do, her
tears turned to hard racking sobs. Of course, she wanted to
see him again; of course, she wanted to go. But she
couldn't stay either. With only a hundred dollars left, she
was in desperate straits. She knew she could sleep in her
car if no one molested her. Yet thoughts of sleeping as a
homeless person sent her into a tailspin. She wasn't a
survivalist, she was just a scared, destitute woman with no
skills or desire to sleep in a box, under a tree, or foraging
off the land. It was time to get real, forget dreaming about
someone she would never be.

Looking around her, she calculated if she hurried,
she'd be finished packing in a couple of hours. The sooner
she was gone the better. As she packed her books, clothing
and paraphernalia, she reminded herself it had only been a
few short weeks ago she had done the same thing in
Leitchfield. It bothered her to think she was running away
again, but what other choice did she have?

Page tussled and cursed as she manipulated the
boxes into the trunk of her car wondering how she had
accumulated so much in such a short time. In and out, she
carried boxes while Sammy scurried from one corner to
another, aware something was awry. When the door buzzer
rang, she hesitated. Was it the landlord? Michael?

"Page? Are you there? It's Kaitlin."

She let out the breath she'd been holding. Opening the door, in a rather flat tone of voice she said, "Kait, what a nice surprise."

"Don't sound so happy to see me. I'm on my way to the feed store. Thought I'd drop in and see you if that's all right."

"Sure. Um, could we talk outside?" Page blocked Kait from coming through the door.

"Why? What's going on? Is this a bad time?" Kait tried peering around Page.

Tears pooled in her eyes. Page slumped, backing away to let Kait enter. She was glad to see Kait; she was like the sister Page never had. She could talk to Kait and confide in her knowing it would go no farther. It warmed her to think Kaitlin had come to see her, especially when she had been so delinquent in keeping in touch.

"What are you doing?" Kait stumbled over Sammy as he ran from wall to wall as if loco on catnip.

"Moving," she said, sniffing and wiping her nose with her hand.

Kait raised her eyebrows. "Where to?"

Shrugging her shoulders, she said, "Probably some street corner." Salty tears rolled down her cheeks. Quickly she swiped them away, ashamed at letting Kait see her cry.

"Page, I may be overstepping my bounds, but I think there's something you desperately need to talk about. I want you to know I'm here for you."

That was the frosting on the cake. Page needed a sisterly shoulder to cry on. Page spilled her guts while Kaitlin sat quietly listening. When Page had exhausted her woes, Kaitlin gave her a hug. "Well, girl, you certainly are a dreamer. Mountain men went out years ago. Of course, a few hearty men still like to project that image. And open range is passé. Traipsing around on someone's land could get you shot or in jail. Why on earth do you want to be like a mountain man?"

"Freedom. Strength. I never had any with Michael. I felt like I was imprisoned. I just want to be self-sufficient, strong, capable of doing things without leaning on someone else. I want to be different than what I am."

"Page, honey, freedom you have. You divorced Michael. You 'roamed' all the way out here, and you're making your way. Just because you haven't found a job yet doesn't mean you're not self-sufficient or strong. You're stronger than you think. Rather than go traipsing off, why not come live with me for a while?"

Page shook her head. "No, no. I've imposed on the Kincaids too much already."

"I insist. You won't find work in Aladdin either, and you're a good thirty miles away from Rapid City. However, I'm sure you can find a job there, and you're welcome to live with me until you get on your feet. Rent free. You cook and clean."

"That's exactly what I mean. How can I ever be self-sufficient if I buckle and take you up on your offer?" She sniffed.

"Everyone can use a little help now and then. Don't be so hard on yourself. Now I insist you come to the house at least until you can save up some money."

Page could not believe the offer. Why were people so nice out here? Or was it just the Kincaid's? In Leitchfield, people didn't have the time of day for another person's problems; they would have left her for homeless. Talking things over with Kait was therapeutic. Brightening at the thought she could stay in Wyoming a little longer, Page finished packing, more optimistic than she'd been in weeks.

True to her words, within two weeks of moving in with Kaitlin, Page found work in Rapid City as a receptionist. The weight of her financial burden eased knowing she had a job, although she felt far from solvent. In addition to her day job, Page did most of the cooking and cleaning while Kait busied herself with maintenance, laundry, helping Quaid and caring for the neighbor's horses. However, Page wished she could trade places with her; she'd much rather be at the ranch learning what she could about the land, the horses, the cattle. And being around a certain brown-eyed cowboy.

* * * *

One day while Page was rolling out a crust for an apple pie and Kaitlin was passing through the kitchen on her way to the laundry room, Page's curiosity got the best of her and she ventured to ask, "Kaitlin? How do you manage? You don't have a job. . ."

Kaitlin set the laundry basket down. She leaned her frame against the countertop. "Well, most ranches pass down from family member to family member. Often, inheritance covers things. Sometimes the sale of cattle gets us through. Other times we're in deep debt. And you should know by now my peanut butter sandwiches and hot dog lunches mean we live close to the bone. Now I'm not saying we don't have day jobs either. There's plenty who do and still work late into the night ranching. Caring for Charlie's horses give me spending money. The rest was inheritance."

"So this was your parents' home?"

"Yes. When Dad got too old for ranching, they moved here. When they passed on, Quaid and I split the inheritance. I had enough for this place, which is just a rural home, with no real acreage. I live frugal. A couple pair of jeans, a pair of boots, and a few groceries. I have enough to pay the taxes and utilities. Now, Quaid. . . " She wondered if she should tell Page about Quaid's failed marriage, about the solvency of the ranch.

"So, Quaid. . . ?" Page prodded Kait to continue.

"Quaid's had to fight for everything he owns."

"If it's that rough, that lean, why live here?"

Kaitlin laid down the towel she was folding as her brown eyes glazed over. "It's the land, Page. It gets into your blood. You start having a relationship with it. I suppose freedom has something to do with it too. I could never live all cramped up in the city; I'd be afraid and claustrophobic."

"Claustrophobic, I understand. But afraid? I'd think you'd be more afraid out here in the middle of nowhere with no one around."

"That's just it, Page. I'm comfortable with myself. I'm not afraid to be by myself. I've got a shotgun and a couple of rifles and my pistol. You can't live out here and not be able to shoot; you never know when a bobcat, mountain lion or a coyote might come 'round after the horses or cattle. Human predators are pretty rare, although you'll always hear about some drunken brawl at one of the bars. Sometimes someone gets shot. Not frequenting bars, I don't have any trouble there. Besides, Charlie Switzer is down the road five miles. Any trouble, I can call him."

Page envied Kaitlin's self-confidence. Maybe if she had a gun she would feel more assured. Pioneer women knew how to shoot guns. Would Quaid teach her how? Where had Kaitlin learned? And where would she get one?

"I've never handled a gun. It kind of scares me. I guess I'm afraid it will go off accidentally and I'll shoot myself."

"No fear as long as the safety is on. You can use mine if you want to learn. If you still think you need one, you could get one from a gun or pawnshop. We'll go out to the gravel pit someday and practice."

Hot dang! Maybe I'll be a western woman yet.

CHAPTER NINE

Thanksgiving and Christmas were fast approaching when Page wondered if she would be included in the Kincaid's holiday plans.

"So, what are you planning for the holidays?" Page asked one evening as she helped Kaitlin fold laundry.

"I forgot all about it. Let me think. Are you going back to Leitchfield?" Kait set aside the laundry to slice into a loaf of banana bread Page had made the night before, then walked into the living room and slumped into a chair.

"To Leitchfield? No way! There's no one there I want to see. My parents died three years ago and Trev and I aren't close like you and Quaid. And I certainly don't want to run into Michael."

"Tell me about Michael, Page."

The look on Page's face darkened. Soberly, she shook her head. "I don't want to talk about him. He's not nice."

Kait eased her lean legs out of the chair, brushed her hair back off her neck, and wandered back into the kitchen. Opening another package of cocoa, she poured it in her cup. She motioned to Page asking if she wanted a refill, before pouring hot tap water in the cup and placing it in the microwave. When it pinged, she took it out and dropped a handful of miniature marshmallows in it before returning to the living room.

"With our parents gone, Quaid and I try to make the holidays special, but only after ranch chores are done. Winter is the slowest time on the ranch, but the cattle need more tending. Lucky that fluke snowstorm ended and there was enough grass left in the pasture. We only had to feed the cattle two days. Now that the snow is so heavy, we're going to have to feed them every day. The horses still need their daily attention and repairs need doing. And then there are all these. . ." She fingered a pile of mail order catalogs multiplying faster than bunny rabbits. "I better look through these or there won't be any gifts under the Christmas tree. I go to Quaid's on Christmas Eve for supper and gifts then spend Christmas day until after chores and noon dinner," she continued. "Why not join us? And bring Trev. No one should be alone on the holidays."

"That's nice of you, but I doubt he'd come. He has a pretty demanding job photographing celebrities. Besides, we're not close. But what about Thanksgiving?"

Kaitlin raised her eyebrows at the prestigious job Trevor held. She turned her head to look at a calendar near the phone. "Thanksgiving, good grief, it's a week away! I guess somebody better go shoot a turkey."

"Shoot one? Why not buy one?" Large turkey farms dotted rural Leitchfield, but Page had never seen or heard of anyone shooting the turkeys. As far as she knew, they were shipped to a processing plant. She'd always bought her turkeys at the grocery store.

"We don't get much turkey out here. Too expensive to ship. Too expensive to buy. Wild turkey's not bad once you get used to it. Of course if you'd rather have venison or antelope. . ."

"I've never had venison. Or any game. Except, buffalo burger." Page knew mountain men lived on game

89

but as a city girl it was never on the menu. Although curious about its taste, the thought of killing a beautiful deer or the caramel and white coated antelope that dotted the plains disturbed her. "Noooooooo, please don't shoot a deer."

"Umm, you don't know what you're missin'. Quaid's got a mean recipe. Not gamey at all. If he had more time, he'd probably get both for the freezer. Well, turkey it is. Want to go with?"

"You mean, you're going to shoot it?" she asked, surprised.

"I could. But I'll check and see what that brother of mine is up to."

The laundry folded and put away, Kaitlin preoccupied herself with her recipe cards. She went on to say, "I'll have to get busy baking. I usually take Charlie a plate of cookies and breads a few days before Christmas. The church always has a cookie exchange. And I've got chokecherry jelly I made earlier this year. But, I guess I better get a Thanksgiving menu planned."

"Oh, let me help," Page cried. "I love to bake and it will occupy these long nights. And let me pay for the sides—mashed potatoes, gravy, what kind of vegetable should we have?" As Kaitlin began shaking her head, Page added, "Please, I've been freeloading too long."

"Nonsense. You haven't stockpiled any money yet. Tell you what. Leave Thanksgiving to me, but yes, you can help with the Christmas baking. Christmas, if you feel you can afford to, you can furnish the meat. Your choice."

Page made a face. "Will I. . .will I have to shoot it?"

Kait laughed. "That's up to you."

*   *   *   *

Page couldn't understand what had happened between her and Quaid. It was as if he had dropped off the face of the earth. No calls. No visits. Kaitlin would have informed him that she was living with her, wouldn't she? As Thanksgiving Day approached, she felt a restless, uneasiness anticipating his reaction at seeing her again. Would he be civil?

When the day came, it was a quiet affair of feeding stock, prayer, dinner and conversation. If he was upset at her being there he didn't let on. He was talkative, but cooler than she thought he needed to be. Was he still mad at her for turning down the Baxter Black date?

Although Page didn't find wild turkey very tasty, she felt proud of herself for trying it. She was also relieved not to be the one who had pulled the trigger killing the poor beast. Apparently, Quaid or Kaitlin had that honor, along with plucking and dressing it.

No longer interested in emulating mountain men or pioneer women her new love was having a ranch. Spending Thanksgiving at the Double K only reinforced the desire.
"I wish I had a ranch," she said wistfully. "I could have all the critters I want: horses, goats, llamas, dogs, and cats. The little wild animals would all be welcome too—bunny rabbits, bobcats, coyotes, porcupines, pikas."

Quaid chuckled when she expressed her longings. "Girl, you don't want a ranch, you want a game preserve."

She looked puzzled.

"You have to understand the animal chain. Out here, certain critters are vermin. We live with 'em, but we don't want any coyotes or prairie dogs. Wolves are bad. Bobcats and mountain lions usually stay more in the mountainous regions, but occasionally come into the grasslands and scrub. They can harm a body or kill cattle, horses, dogs, cats. You've probably read where horses fall into prairie dog holes. Land the wrong way, break a leg. Have to put the horse down. In fact us ranchers kind of look on prairie dogs as a nuisance. Shooting 'em is a sport . . . go out and shoot as many as possible."

"But they're so cute," Page protested. "I like how they pop out of the ground like jack-in-the-boxes."

"Maybe you think so, but they also carry disease."

"Coyotes are just dogs aren't they?" she said, trying another approach.

"From the dog family. But they're big nuisances too. Scavengers. Like I said, if you're going to entertain a menagerie, you need a zoo not a ranch."

"But the mountain men lived with all those animals. The Indians too."

"Mountain men, Indians," he jeered. "You read too many books. This is the 21st century. You'd be better off reading Range or American Cowboy. Besides, coming by a ranch is a tough proposition; you've got to be wealthy enough to afford enough grazing land or come by it through inheritance." As an afterthought, he added, "Or, I guess you've got to be a movie star."

Curious to know how Quaid had obtained his ranch, she asked, "So you got enough inheritance for this spread?"

A dark cloud scudded across his face. "No."

Immediately the day's festivities seemed to take a somber tone.

"Umm, another law of the land, Page. Never ask how much a rancher makes or how big a spread they have or how many cattle. That's personal business. I know you don't know these things and lots of folks wouldn't tell you either, but how else will you learn?" Kait filled in.

"I'm sorry. I didn't know." Contrite, Page aimed her apology at Quaid.

"Yeah, well now you do," he said with annoyance.

Page remembered what Kaitlin told her about Quaid having to fight for everything he owned. Was that why he was so ornery? Was he on the defense all the time? Or was he just overly sensitive?

"I guess I'll never have a ranch. I'm none of those things nor do I have an inheritance. I guess I'm just living out of my time, I mean those times when there was open range and mountain men and all. I guess I'm just a Wyoming dreamer." She sighed.

"Page! Page, wake up!"

Page jerked awake thinking there must be an emergency.

"We're going to get a Christmas tree. Get dressed!"

Page couldn't imagine anyone getting so excited over picking out a tree. It wasn't until after breakfast, Page comprehended it was a big adventure. They were going up in the mountains for the tree. She vaguely remembered her experience in the higher altitudes and hoped Quaid was an excellent driver. Being stranded again would be just too much.

Shortly thereafter, the three jumped into Quaid's truck and headed out County Road Seven. The pickup climbed the snow-covered roads and state lands as the forest of trees thickened. Higher and higher, they climbed, passing swathes of felled timber and manmade timber roads. The big log-hauling semi's made mush of the roads, leaving wide ruts, but Quaid skillfully maneuvered his way around them. As they approached eight thousand feet, Page looked out the window at the steep incline ahead. As Quaid accelerated up the incline, the single lane roadbed turned into deep, icy ruts. It began snowing heavily and the tick-tack-tick-tack of the wipers added to her nervousness.

"Better put 'er in four-wheel drive. We don't want to get stuck out here," Kait said holding on to the dash, peering out at the ruts.

Quaid locked in the four-wheel drive.

Page, wedged between Quaid and Kaitlin, couldn't see how close they were to the mountain's edge, but she could see the road ahead and the drop-off appeared to be no more than a foot wide before heading straight down the mountainside.

"Couldn't you just go to the store for one?" she asked. Nervous, she craned her neck to see out the side windows, then back to the front.

"Store?" he said astonished. "Why would you want a store bought when you can come up here and pick one out yourself?"

"Watch out!" Page yelled as a couple of mule deer ran out ahead of them.

Startled, Quaid turned the wheel just enough that the tires jumped the ruts. The truck shimmied and tires spun before he got the tires back in line. "Damn! Don't do that again," he groused.   "It's them or us."

Page remained silent, catching her breath, chewing at her lips, fretting all the way, not sure, whether her relief was for the deer or for themselves. Her tender heart was spared seeing the animals hurt as they bounded away startled by the mechanized intrusion into their world.

Minutes later, they stopped in what seemed like complete wilderness. Quaid jumped out, grabbed the chain saw from the truck bed, and traipsed off into the woods with Kaitlin at his heels.

When Page stepped out, the quietness of the mountain overwhelmed her. The blowing wind, an occasional slough of snow sliding off branches, or the scurry of birds was the only audible noise other than their footsteps. Had she been alone she would have wanted to go exploring. Hearing their voices in the near distance, Page hurried to join them. Quaid stood before a six-foot tree that looked like something out of a Charlie Brown's Christmas. Although the needles were lush forest green, big gaps of branchless areas glared at her; it was not full like the blue spruce trees she'd had in Christmas' past.

"What do you think, Page?" Kaitlin asked, her breath making clouds in the air.

Page wrinkled up the corner of her lip. "Looks kinda puny to me. There's not enough branches."

"City girl—this is a real tree, not those tree farm things," Quaid explained. "Just wait 'til we get it inside and the smell of cedar fills the room." He revved the saw, and in minutes, the three of them lifted it into the truck bed.

Zing! A snowball came whizzing past Page by inches. Locating its source, she stooped down, scooped up a handful of snow, packed it and wound up her arm like a pro ball player. It hit Quaid with a wallop. Not to be outdone, he returned her volley. Soon Kaitlin joined in. The threesome ran and ducked one another's snowballs, laughing and yelling like elementary school kids in the cold mountain air.

Breathless, Kait climbed back into the truck. "We'll decorate it when we get back to the Double K."

They spent the remainder of the afternoon decorating the tree with simple ornaments of homey materials—cranberry garlands, bandanna bows, and little rope lariats Kaitlin had made one year from sisal.

Memories of Christmas holidays back in Leitchfield flickered through Page's mind: The thousands of dollars in expensive glass ornaments and garland, the lavish room decorations, Michael's friends coming in for drinks and appetizers, followed by a dinner out at the country club, where she had to dress to the nines. . . Out here, it was casual, much quieter, and more spiritual.

Page busied herself in the days before Christmas working, helping Kaitlin with baking, and buying presents. She hadn't heard from Quaid since the tree cutting. Page wondered if he resented her involvement in Kincaid traditions.

Christmas turned into a repeat of Thanksgiving with the exception that Page went all out providing not only a ham, but also side dishes, dessert and bottles of White Zinfandel and Asti Spumante. She wore a royal blue velveteen pantsuit only to find the Kincaids dressed casually in sweaters and jeans. After dinner, they exchanged gifts while listening to Christmas music. Quaid and Kaitlin gave her a pair of Sorel boots. She gave Kaitlin a gorgeous raspberry colored sweater, and Quaid two tickets to see Waddy Mitchell, another cowboy poet, in the hope he would ask her to go with him, but it didn't prompt an invite.

After a big breakfast Christmas morning, Kaitlin and Quaid filled the bed of the pickup with hay. Page stayed behind to wash dishes while the Kincaids checked and fed the cattle. By mid-afternoon, the weather turned into a wintry squall. After a noon meal of leftovers, the gals cleaned things up, before leaving in the blinding snow for Aladdin.

*   *   *   *

The following day, Page barely got to her desk at Siler, Jones and Krauthammer, Attorneys at Law, when she received a phone call.

"Kait's been in an accident. She's in the hospital here in Rapid," Quaid said.

"Noooo, is she alright?"

"Broken leg, cracked rib, some other minor injuries they say. Surgery is at 10 a.m. this morning."

Page promptly called a florist and had flowers sent to Kaitlin's room, and then made a mental note to stop in on her lunch hour and see how she was doing.

"Oh, my gosh. Are you going to be all right?" Page asked walking into the hospital room seeing all the paraphernalia hooked up to Kaitlin.

Kait shifted uneasily in the leg harness. "It's going to take time. It was still snowing hard when I left for Quaid's. I swerved to avoid a "muley", a mule deer, and didn't see the other car until it was too late. Now look at me. I'm useless to Quaid and he's going to need help." She winced as a spasm of pain went through her.

"I could help," Page offered. "Tomorrow's the weekend."

"Umm, I don't know. It's pretty rough. You better call Charlie. Charlie Switzer. He might be willing to help Quaid. He's going to need help longer than just the weekend."

"Please let me try. If it wasn't for me needing to get back to work today, you could have stayed at the ranch. Then none of this would have happened."

"It's not up to me. You'll need to ask Quaid. He just left. I'm surprised you didn't run into him. Maybe he'd let you drive the pickup. You have to keep an eye on the range and the other in the rear view mirror. Quaid will motion where he wants you to go." Kait sunk into the bed, her eyes closing.

"That's simple enough. I'll call him and tell him I'll be there."

"He'll expect you no later than five."

Page groaned. "I know. Ranchers never sleep in late, do they?" She chuckled. "Oh well, I think I'm getting used to it."

When she returned to the office, she tried several times to contact Quaid. When he finally answered, she practically had to badger him before he gave in. The remainder of the day, Page could barely concentrate on her duties her anticipation was so great.

97

CHAPTER TEN

"Let's go. You drive. I'll feed. You're going to have to watch me. I'll—"

"I know. Kait filled me in." She zipped her jacket and tugged at the hood strings.

Backing the pickup to the barn, Quaid filled the bed with bale after bale. When it was stacked four high, he sat atop a bale and motioned Page out of the barn. Bumping over frozen cow patties, Page jostled in the seat while keeping a watchful eye for signals from Quaid. The first couple of motions confused her causing her to turn left when she should have turned right.

"Watch out!" He yelled.

Page slammed on the brakes just short of hitting a yearling running in front of the truck. When she looked back, Quaid was gone! Within seconds, he limped to the driver's door ranting and raving.

"Are you trying to kill me? Don't ever slam on the brakes like that. Maybe you'd like to switch places. Here's a quick lesson. Pay attention. Grab a bale. Cut the twine. Dump it over the edge. Got it?"

She nodded assent. Contrite, she offer an apology. However, he either didn't hear it or was ignoring her. He climbed back into the truck forcing her to exit on the passenger side.

Page shifted her weight in the truck bed to counterbalance as they jostled over rough ground. As Quaid slowed to a crawl, she watched for his signal. She grabbed, grunted, pulled, and finally pushed with her knees struggling to get the bale over the tailgate. "Oh, rats! I forgot to cut the twine. Quaid! Quaid!" she called out for him to stop, but he didn't hear her. Suddenly she had the idea if she cut the twine ahead of time it might help. She grabbed a bale, her wool gloves snagging on the binding. Yanking them off hastily, she cut the twine, ready to dump the next time he gave the signal. However, when he did, the bundle crumbled and flaked apart. Page scooped up what she could by the handfuls tossing it overboard leaving a Hansel and Gretel trail behind.

Before she could work her gloves out of the baling twine, he was motioning again. This time the binding twine cut into her hands. Scooting the bale to the edge, she cut the twine, and then giving it a swift boot she promptly landed on her behind. Swiping at a trickle of sweat on her forehead, she righted herself just as Quaid zagged to the left causing her to topple over again. Rubbing at the tender bruised areas it left on her shoulder and hip, she missed his cue to dump. A few yards out he motioned again. This time she got the bale to the edge of the tailgate and cut the twine, but a wind blew up and spewed the hay back into the truck. Over and over Page tried to lift the bales with each one heavier than the last.

As they came back to the barn, Page studied her wind-chapped hands, the broken fingernails she had just nicely grown out, and two, three small cuts. Her face itched and as she threw the hood of her jacket back she could feel twigs of hay in her hair. She stood brushing the chaff off her clothes when Quaid came around to the end of the pickup. "What the —"

"What's so funny?" she asked.

"You. You look like a scarecrow."

Page started to laugh then noticed his dark, dour side clouding his face.

Seeing how many bales remained in the truck bed, he turned aside, grumbling, ". . . should've known a greenhorn couldn't handle this. Get out. I'll do this myself. Don't worry. I'll get Charlie to help tomorrow."

"No, Quaid, I said I'd help and I will." Feeling punished for trying to be helpful, she spat quietly, "I bet you weren't perfect the first time either." He must have heard her as she watched him bristle. "Can't you have patience with me? I'm trying." She bent forward and backward trying to get the crick out of her back.

He grimaced. "Oh, all right. You can drive the truck. Just no sudden stops and pay attention. What's the matter?"

"Just a sore back. Those bales are heavy."

"If you live out here, you're going to have a few aches and pains. Comes with the territory." He raised his hand to help her down off the truck bed.

". . . guess I can't do anything right," she mumbled, as she dragged her feet, heading to the house.

Quaid caught up with her, grabbing her arm. He spun her around to face him. "You're going to give up just like that? Rule #1: Cowboy up. Face your failure. Brush yourself off and try again. No one does everything right the first time around."

"But you just said—"

"Never mind what I said. Let's go get warmed up with a cup of coffee. Afterwards we'll try it again. You drive. I'll feed."

After coffee and upon returning to the barn the second time, Page parked the truck and got out. "How'd I do?" she asked, anticipating a positive response.

Unemotional, he answered, "You'll do," as he gathered up baling twine and cutters.

"That's all?" She stood by the truck, disappointed he wasn't more encouraging.

"Yeah, that's all." A sly smile creased the corners of his mouth as he dropped the twine and cutters, scooped up a handful of hay and tossed it at her.

"Hey! No fair," she squealed, reading his action as playful and teasing. She scrabbled to the truck bed for a handful to return the act.

Before she could fling it at him, he came up behind her. When she whirled around, their bodies nearly touched. She paused while he studied her a moment. She felt his calloused hand brush her hair back from her face as he picked out a piece of hay. What should she to do? She looked at him but couldn't read him. He still looked severe. Then his hand curved around the softness of her cheek. She knew she should pull away, but something held her motionless. His touch sent a little quiver of ecstasy through her. He leaned in closer, his warm breath caressing her cold, wind-chafed face. Her eyes darted from his eyes to his cheek to his chin and back to his eyes. He was so close to her. Would he kiss her? Slowly, he moved toward her lips. Aware of his body heat, she closed her eyes, her knees weakened. She felt like the melting witch in Oz as she waited for his kiss.

No whiskers scratched her delicate skin, no warm breath caressed her, no wet lips touched hers. Opening her eyes, she watched him turn away, heading to the barn to return cutters to the nail peg. She stood there for a moment trying to figure what had just transpired between them.

Whoo! That was a close call. Page had stood proudly in front of him awaiting affirmation, hay in her hair and chaff all over her. She looked cute all messed up.

However, when he saw her exuberant, expectant face fall with his choice of words, he knew she'd taken him too seriously. With a playful toss of hay at her, her entire countenance changed; her face came alive. The wind-chafed hue in her cheeks accentuated her blue eyes now dancing with teasing and laughter. Her face was radiant and glowing. Beautiful. Desirable. At that moment, he wanted to take her in his arms, hold her, and feel her soft curves against him. Kiss her. He'd come so close. But he couldn't. If he did, he'd want more, and if she responded the way he thought . . . well, it just couldn't happen.

His feelings amok since their rodeo date, he'd been torn between seeing her again and keeping his distance. After turning him down on their second date with no explanation he wondered if perhaps their rodeo date hadn't went as well as he thought. Yet she had no problem joining in their holiday traditions. She was a hard one to figure out. Now with Kaitlin laid up, he'd be seeing Page everyday if he allowed it. Finding her attractiveness distracting and her close proximity sexually arousing, Quaid found it hard to stick to his resolve. He was even beginning to question if he wanted to. On the other hand, even if he could trust her and work with her, he couldn't afford to wrap himself around her as he'd done with Denise.

He gave her credit though. Lifting and breaking a hay bale was no easy task. Yet she'd jumped at the chance. Afterwards, he'd noticed her cut hands. Waiting for her to whine and complain, she'd never said a word. He remembered her helping Kaitlin muck out stalls with only a mere mention of ruining her jeans. He thought back to Thanksgiving, to her remark about wanting a ranch and her love of animals. Maybe it was something; or maybe it was nothing. Was Page Chandling the kind of woman he was looking for?

It was apparent Page seemed eager to please, yet he knew that eagerness could wear away all too soon; the daily grind of ranching wore thin in no time. A few women actually enjoyed it, but it was hard, often dangerous work. Monotonous. It was getting up early and going to bed late. Hit and miss meals. Heavy lifting. Injuries. The neighboring ranchers all talked about how their wives worried about the endless debt and why anyone would want to be a rancher. For men, he knew it was something in the blood. It was an attachment to the land. Like a drunk addicted to alcohol, the rancher was addicted to the land, the cattle, freedom, and work. Ranching was in his blood and he wasn't about to trade it for Page Chandling. Not for a minute.

Busting bales had been rough, hard work. Her hands were stiff, swollen and sore; the cuts stung. Her back ached and she felt like she'd pulled a muscle. *How do these people do this every day?* She knew she hadn't done it as well as Kaitlin, but she'd felt exhilarated trying. If only Quaid could see that. If he could see her willingness to learn, to jump in and do whatever was expected of her.

Feeding the cattle wasn't as much fun or as easy as feeding Chester, Blue and Sammy, but if the job wasn't done the cattle would starve. She would never want to be a part of deliberately causing death to any animal. Confident she could learn to do it properly, she hoped tomorrow would be a better day.

When she returned to Kaitlin's, she found a heating pad to be just the thing for her sore back. While she lay soaking in the soothing heat, she relived her playful moment with Quaid; it brought a warm glow to her heart and a smile to her lips. It was wonderful seeing him lighten up having fun. Had he been teasing or was it some kind of foreplay to his deeper feelings? After a half hour on the heating pad, she took a hot bath and then fell asleep, although it was only mid-day.

The following morning in spite of wind, snow, and sore, cracked hands, she pulled into the drive of the Double K. She trudged to the barn like a trooper and offered to do the feeding, but Quaid insisted on doing it himself. As she bumped along through the pasture, she wondered if something similar to yesterday's playfulness would happen again today. When they had completed the pass through the pasture and approached the house, Quaid suggested she make some cocoa while he put tools away.

Handing a steaming cup to Quaid as he came in, she said, "I can be here tomorrow before work. We can be done early enough that I won't have to call in late, don't you think?" She sipped at the hot chocolate, feeling its warmth run through her.

"You could spend the night."

His response gave her such a start she choked on the hot chocolate. A nervous tremor went through her. Was he suggesting what she thought he might be suggesting? They hadn't even kissed! Although pleased at the thought of getting to know Quaid better, she couldn't help but question his asking her to sleep over. She certainly wasn't ready to jump into bed with him. That always seemed to entangle all her feelings, all her plans. For men it was simple; it was sex. Why couldn't they separate the two?

No matter. She was going to be self-sufficient. She didn't need a man.

"Not this time," she murmured. *Oh cripes, why did I say that? That implies I'm willing at another time.* Did she mean to give him hope? Her cheeks felt on fire as warmth spread through her.

Changing the subject, she said, "What'd you ever do with those Waddy Mitchell tickets?" Page asked. "I was thinking we could eat at the Golden Eagle and then go to the concert." She bit her tongue. The Golden Eagle was the most posh restaurant in the area. It was the kind of place

104

Michael would take her to. Price meant nothing to him. But maybe Quaid couldn't afford it.

"Guess I forgot about 'em. I'm not even sure where they are anymore."

Refusing to be discouraged, she said, "Let's look for them. I have the rest of the day." She meandered around lifting up magazines, checking the roll-top desk and when she didn't find anything in plain sight, she said, "Why don't you check your clothes in the mudroom? I'll check the bedrooms."

Page, on hands and knees, peered for the tickets under Quaid's bed.

"Not there," he said walking in the bedroom to see her on all fours. The pose was too provocative; he felt the growing bulge in his jeans.

"Don't just stand there, help me," she said, flattening herself out, before rising back up in a cat stretch.

He squatted near her, resting on his heels.

Page shifted and felt herself losing her balance. She bumped into him the same time her knees buckled. Falling over, it knocked him off balance with both of them falling sideways. Awkwardly positioned, thinking he needed leverage to get up, she twisted around to face him. His hand skimmed her breast before finding purchase on her waist. She looked in his face finding it softened, different than she had ever seen before. Face to face, their warm breaths intermingled as they eyed each other expectantly. Bodies touching. She paused. His hand slid up her side, up to her breast, and then he was cupping it, kneading it gently, drawing her closer. Her breath quickened. How far would this go? She placed her hand on his hip and one on his chest as if to resist him, but the rising heat in her didn't push him away. His hand came up to her throat, her jaw line. She felt his fingers tilt her jaw for a better angle, saw the desire in his eyes, heard his heavy breathing, felt his warm lips draw near. As she closed her eyes, she slipped away into his tender kiss. She felt him break away, but before she could open her eyes, he was kissing her again. Stronger, deeper, longer. Page gave a little moan of pleasure.

At the sound of her moan, he broke away. *What am I doing?* With a full erection the easiest thing to do would be make love to her. He opted for the hardest. Almost in pain, he fumbled to rise, leaving her there on the floor, while he made his way to the bathroom, where he jacked off as he had done so many times in the past.

Relieved, he returned to the bedroom filled with remorse. "I'm sorry, Page. I don't know what I did with them." Expecting her to be chagrined, he found her in the spare bedroom—the one she used to recuperate. She held the tickets in her hands. Rather than elation at finding them, her body was rigid, her face drawn tight.

"Hey, you found them."

"Sorry? Sorry I found them? In the wastebasket! They obviously meant nothing to you." Her lips quivered. Tears formed at the corners of her eyes.

"The wastebasket? How'd they get there?" He walked towards her to take the tickets from her hands.

"You tell me!"

He stood nonplussed watching her tear them into little pieces, before flinging them in the air and storming past him.

"Page, wait. Let me explain." Where had he heard those words before? He took after her finding her walking to the barn.

"Page, honey, listen." He grabbed her by the arm, twirling her around. She was crying. Damn. He hadn't meant to upset her. "C'mere, Page." He pulled her into his arms. "I'm sorry, Page. I didn't throw them away. I swear. They must have fallen off the nightstand or out of my clothes or something. I swear I didn't throw them away.

They were a great Christmas gift. I really wanted them. I did." As her tears eased, he pushed her slightly away so he could look in her face. "Ya think we could piece 'em together?"

The thought of joining the little pieces scattered on the floor took on an amused picture in her mind as her tears ceased and the corners of her mouth curled up into a shy smile.

Moments later sitting at the kitchen table, she said, "It's no use. They're ruined." She drew back in the chair. "I'm sorry, Quaid." Seeing the let down look on his face, she added, "That was mean of me. I shouldn't have done that. I guess I just wanted to hurt you because I was hurt."

"Maybe they'd accept them anyway. We could try."

"If they won't, I've ruined a perfect evening. Forgive me?"

"Yeah. They're just tickets. We could still go out to eat. Forgive me?"

"Forgive you? For what?"

"I'm sorry for just leaving you on the floor a few minutes ago. I didn't want things goin' too far, just bein' friends an' all."

Friends? She didn't realize they were even on that level. Then she remembered he had called her honey. A ripple of pleasure ran through her. Was the iceman softening? He'd finally kissed her. And she wanted more. What was happening? Maybe not all men were scum after all.

* * * *

Page loved her days at the Double K wishing she could be there all the time. The work was strenuous but fulfilling. The cold mountain air invigorating in spite of the workload that caused her to sweat. No longer afraid of Blue and Chester dashing about her, she was even overcoming her fear of the cattle and horses. Of all the tasks, she found she loved currying the horses until their coats shined. One day she hoped Quaid would let her ride.

In spite of loving the ranch and all she was learning, she reminded herself she needed her job at Siler, Jones and Krauthammer. She needed to add to her rainy day fund if she was ever to get out from Kaitlin's hospitality. Her savings was compounding nicely although she felt guilty not paying room and board.

After work, Page stopped in the hospital to visit Kaitlin and monitor her progress.

"How's it going with my brother?" Kait asked, struggling to stand up with the aide of a nurse.

"Fine. Boy, I never knew how hard ranching was. Between getting up at three or four to feed the cattle, change clothes and come in to work, stopping in to see you, going home and doing what needs doing, it's a long day. I'm so pooped all I want to do is go to bed."

"Is Charlie taking care of my horse? What about his horses? Has he said anything about my not being there?" Kait teetered as a nurse held on to her.

"Don't worry. He's taking care of his horses and Brandy. I've been watching him with her, and I think I could brush her down and feed her."

"I'd like that, but I don't want you taking on too much."

"Quaid's let me curry the horses at the ranch. I know how now. I could do Brandy."

"I'm sure you could, but I think you've got enough on your plate at the moment." Changing thought, she added, "I am going to miss my income from Charlie though. Oh well, I'll find a way to manage. Is Quaid still being rude to you?"

"Umm, yes and no. I think he might be mellowing a tad. Or I'm getting used to him."

"You've got it bad for him, haven't you?" Kaitlin could not teeter on her broken leg any longer and fell back against the bed. The nurse helped her get back in the bed before making a note on her chart, then leaving the room.

"Pretty obvious, huh?" Page flushed. *Is it obvious to Quaid?* "Your brother is umm, interesting . . . sometimes nice. And you know, I love being out at the ranch. It's just. . ."

"Just what? Nothing's happening?" Kait waited for reaction from Page.

Page nodded although it felt like a lie. Hadn't Quaid finally kissed her? Hadn't he invited her to spend the night? And what about herself? When had she chucked her resolve never to get involved with another man? Flashes of Quaid's quick mood swings passed through her mind. Was she neglecting the signs of an abuser? Or was Quaid naturally dour? Maybe she was expecting too much too soon.

Kait relaxed into the mattress. "I've been thinking, Page. Maybe you need to expand your horizons. I think you're lonely, Page. Why don't you try going to church? It's always a good place to meet a man."

To meet a man? She didn't want to meet a man. She was enraptured with Quaid Kincaid. Disappointed, she asked, "Are you telling me your brother has no interest in me?"

"All I can say is my brother's been hurt bad. He's dated a couple of times, but he doesn't get serious about anyone. The ranch is his sole focus."

"All work and no play make Quaid a dull boy. What, or who, hurt him?" Page sat down on the edge of the bed near Kaitlin.

"Sorry. If you want to know, you'll have to ask him yourself." She winced as the added pressure on the bed caused some pain.

"Geez! You Kincaids sure are a tight lipped bunch."

* * * *

So, Quaid doesn't get serious about anyone. Was she just dreaming their kiss meant something? Maybe Kaitlin was right. Maybe she was just lonely and picking on Quaid to fill the void. Maybe being around other people would help. When Sunday rolled around, Page rushed home from the ranch to change into one of her prettiest dresses and high-heeled boots. She affixed some gold dangle earrings to her earlobes, snapped on a gold bracelet, and worked over thirty minutes on her makeup and hair. She grabbed up a faux rabbit fur coat she'd bought at a thrift store and headed out the door.

Driving into Sundance looking for a place of worship, Page thought back to when she last entered a church. It had been years. Michael thought it a waste of time and if it was a waste of time for him, it was a waste of time for her.

She parked her car across the street from the white board church. Approaching the double doors, she almost turned around having second thoughts. However, a woman in a turquoise suede, ankle-length dress and a puffy down filled jacket held the door open for her saying, "Good Morning, we're glad you're here." Committed to going through with it, she entered the First Baptist Church.

As she stood in the hall, she looked over the already seated crowd. The women wore little makeup. Their clothing was subdued and very little jewelry adorned them. Suede, nylon pile, or wool coats hung over the women's shoulders. It was clear she was overly dressed. Embarrassed, she slipped her bracelet into her coat pocket. With a Kleenex, she pretended to wipe her nose, but actually wiped off most of her lipstick. Although the little church was drafty, she left her coat in the narthex.

110

"Is this seat taken?" she whispered, purposely walking up to a pew with a lone man dressed in a western cut shirt, crisp clean blue jeans, and a leather vest.

Without a word, he shifted in the pew making more room for her.

Out of the corner of her eye she glanced at him and when he returned the gaze she buried herself in the bulletin. She judged him to be about six feet tall. His long legs filled the space between the pews making it impossible to pass through unless he stood up. A big man but not overweight. Large, rough hands. Turning her head ever so slightly, she noticed his salt and pepper walrus style moustache covering most of his ruddy face. Sandy red hair peeked out from his sable colored Stetson. *Not exactly a flip-flopping heart throb.*

She scanned the conglomerate of men and women, some with small children by their sides, others with teenagers. Most of the men wore jeans, something unthinkable back in Leitchfield. Some of them had cowboy hats on while others had taken them off. The women wore nice dresses, although a few wore pantsuits. A few wore high heels, but most of them wore cowboy boots.

The congregation conversed noisily, the women shaking hands and men patting one another on the back. Disconcerted at the raucousness, she kept glancing around wondering why these people were so irreverent; she came from a religious background that practiced entering the church in a quiet, worshipful manner. This sounded like a picnic.

Feeling ill at ease if she didn't say something to the man sitting beside her, she turned to him and whispered, "I'm new here. Is it always this noisy?"

"This isn't noisy, ma'am. This is fellowship. We live so far apart from one another, when we get together we have to catch up on things," he said in a deep, strong voice.

"Oh." She turned back, flipping to the backside of the bulletin to read the list of weekly activities. She noticed a singles group met on Friday nights. Should she? Was she that desperate?

She cleared her throat. Leaning towards the man, she again asked, "Do you know anything about this singles group thing on Fridays?"

"Yeah, I do. I've been a couple of times. They try to plan activities where singles can get together. The next thing is a snowmobile party next week. Do you snowmobile?"

Reflecting, she hadn't led a very exciting or adventurous life, she shook her head and with a deflated voice said, "No, I've never been on a snowmobile."

Abruptly he sat up a little straighter and looked her over. "Never?"

She shook her head again.

"Why not come? We go in teams. I'm sure you'll get teamed up with someone with experience. I'm Jake. Jake Stoner." He extended his hand.

"Page Chandling." She smiled, shaking his hand just as the introit began.

*   *   *   *

Released three days from the hospital, Kaitlin hobbled on her crutches to the ringing telephone. "She's not here, Quaid." She wondered what her brother would say or do if he knew she had joined the singles group at the local Baptist Church. Should she tell him? Knowing her brother's jealous streak made her bite her tongue from divulging Page's whereabouts.

"Yeah, sure, you know I'm always available during calving. Page would probably be available too," she told her brother, holding the phone by her chin and shoulder while balancing on the crutches.

112

"I don't know, sis. Calves always seem to come at two or three in the morning. She's a city girl. Never exposed to anything like this it might be too much for her. She seems pretty sensitive."

Exasperated and frustrated with her brother, she said, "Why can't you cut her some slack? She's crazy about you and she wants to live on a ranch more than anything." Kait quickly realized she had said more than she should have.

The phone went silent. Quaid's terse words followed. "Yeah, right. We'll see. . ."

"It was so exciting, Kait. I never imagined I'd like it, but sailing through the snow like that. It's just exhilarating." Page flushed with excitement as she peeled off layers of clothing, then sat down to rub her cold feet. "I was paired up with Jake Stoner. He's the guy I told you about. He's like a giant, but he's such a gentleman. He never made me feel stupid or anything," she raved.

"Sounds like you had a good time." Kait continued scouring for something in the refrigerator.

"Next week, we're going to Barnaby's in Rapid."

"Barnaby's huh? I thought you weren't the bar type." She pulled out a bowl, lifted the tin foil off, and sniffed the contents before closing the refrigerator. She set the bowl on the counter while she searched out a small plate, and then dumped out a portion of macaroni salad. She sat down at the table and continued nibbling away while Page talked.

As if caught in a lie, Page cowered. "I-I'm not. But Jake said it's not a dark, pool hall type bar. It's a nice gathering place. And he said I don't have to drink if I don't want to."

"You don't have to explain to me, Page. You're of age to do whatever you want. Have you met anyone other than Jake?"

"Well, there's Brenda and Larry and Tina and Kyle, but they've kind of hitched up with each other, so they're not exactly singles anymore. They're not married of course, but you know what I mean. There are a couple of other guys in the group, but I haven't really talked to them. Jake seems to always be around."

"Sounds like Jake has taken a shine to you. Do you like Jake?" Kait studied her to see her reaction.

"He's nice." As an afterthought, she added, "But he's not a heart throb."

"Like Quaid?" Kait raised an eyebrow.

Page blushed.

"Listen, calving is coming up. Don't be alarmed if the phone rings in the middle of the night. Sometimes the mother has a rough delivery. I volunteered our services. I thought you wouldn't mind." Kait looked for a sign of approval from Page.

"Calving? Ohhh, I'd love to see a newborn calf."

"It's not for the squeamish."

"Sure, I'm up for it. You know I want to learn everything I can about ranching." Excitement danced in her blue eyes.

*   *   *   *

Two weeks later, Page sat across from Jake at the swingiest nightspot in Rapid. She no longer said Rapid City; natives knocked off the city part. Barnaby's was a casual place filled with round oak tables and captain's chairs. A distressed maple plank floor scuffed with boot marks led to an open dance area. The lighting was soft, not dark, just dimly lit. A huge oak bar sat against one wall with a huge mirror behind it reflecting an assortment of

114

liquor bottles and two-gallon jars filled with pickled eggs. Peanuts sat in baskets on the bar and tables. Animated voices drowned out the country music playing in the background.

Page scanned the room taking in the surroundings, noticing the men mainly wore tight jeans, western shirts, some with leather vests, cowboy boots and hats. Most of them kept their hats on. The women dressed in what Page called prairie fashion: long skirts to their ankles, ruffled or plain blouses, wide Concho style belts, and some wore fancy jackets. Most of the women wore cowboy boots also. Feeling out of place with her clingy sweater dress and high heels, she wished someone had told her how to dress. Her Leitchfield outfit was definitely all wrong. She was going to have to buy some new clothes. Thank goodness, for the time being, she could hide behind the table.

Jake slid his arm around her shoulder, telling her about a funny incident, when she heard a familiar voice.

"Can I have this dance?"

Startled, she looked up to see Quaid hovering over her. Unsure as to what to do or say, she turned to Jake for some kind of answer.

"It's a free country," he said, removing his arm.

Page walked to the dance floor suddenly aware of the upbeat country tune. She didn't know how to dance to this. She'd make a fool of herself and embarrass Quaid. Just then, the music shifted to a slow number. As she felt Quaid's arm circle her waist a lick of flame went up her back. She fit her opposite hand in his and purposely stepped back. If she got too close to him, she might melt with desire. But with the first step Quaid took, his arm tugged at her waist, pulling her closer to him. As he drew her near him, she turned her head to look away and stiffened.

"Hey, relax. I don't bite," he said, just as she stepped on his foot, throwing them out of sync.

115

As he tried to right her, she miss-stepped again and ended up shuffling two, three steps to the right, the momentum almost causing her to fall over. Embarrassed and red faced, she apologized profusely and murmured, "Can we just sit down?"

"It's okay. Try again," he murmured in her ear, pulling her close to him again.

Self-conscious, all she wanted to do was disappear. Try as she might she could not relax in his arms. Thinking everyone must be looking at her clumsy efforts, she pulled away and frantically searched out the sign for the ladies room. Once inside the confines, a wave of nausea overtook her and she thought she would vomit. Shaking, she wet a paper towel and held it to her face. *What a clutz I am. I never should have come here. What must people be thinking? Jake had to see me bumble things. Surely, he won't dare ask me to dance . . . And Quaid. What if Quaid is waiting for me? What should I do?* Several minutes passed as she tried to calm herself and make herself presentable once again.

"Are you okay, Page?" Tina asked cracking open the door. Upon seeing Page's pale face, she came into the restroom. "You kind of left the guys in the lurch."

Saying the first thing to pop into her mind, she replied, "I-I'm sick. I think I should go home. Could you take me home?"

"I think Jake would be glad to take you home if you truly feel that bad. Is it the flu?"

"I dunno." Embarrassed by lying and not wanting to face Jake or Quaid, Page wet the paper towel again and draped her face.

"C'mon. I'll explain to Jake." She put her arm around Page and led her out to the table where Jake stood with a worried look on his face. After Tina explained Page wanted to go home, Jake grabbed his cowboy hat, and flipped through his wallet to pay the tab, just as Quaid came over to the table.

"What's wrong?" Quaid asked looking at Page.

"She's sick. I'm taking her home," Jake said taking a hold of Page's arm to guide her through the crowd.

"No need for you to miss all the fun, cowboy. She lives with my sister. I can take her home." He came close enough to take hold of her other arm.

"She's my date," Jake said, looking Quaid squarely in the face.

"Not quite," Quaid's steely reply was icy cold. He tugged at Page.

"Page?" Holding firm, Jake sought affirmation which one of them she wanted to leave with.

Page stood weakly looking from one to the other wishing she could drop through the floorboards. Thoughts of Michael flicked through her mind; Michael would have started a fight, afterward blaming her later for the entire situation. Was there going to be a barroom brawl right here? As the anxiety of the situation rose within her, she began feeling faint; she thought she heard herself say "Jake" just before going limp.

CHAPTER ELEVEN

Days past. Quaid turned the calendar on the kitchen wall to February. Had it been three weeks since he'd shown up at Barnaby's? Three weeks since Page left him looking like a fool out on the dance floor? If it hadn't been for Kaitlin's cajoling, he never would have went in the first place. When Page walked in with that ruddy faced, mustachioed cowboy it rankled.

"What did you expect? Jake was her date. Maybe you should have asked her out," Kaitlin had said listening to his tale of woe the next day.

After calming down and thinking about it, Page hadn't done anything wrong. If anything, he had to admire her. She stuck by her date, coming and leaving with him, just as he would want it if he were in Jake's shoes. In fact, he thought of her often since their dinner-concert date had never materialized.

Now it was February, calving time. There would be no chance of seeing her until the heifers had dropped their calves. Unable to be away from the ranch, checking cows was an around the clock operation. Heifers needed checking every three, four hours. A cow could get into real trouble if the calf was breech; it would need human intervention to deliver.

That night, Quaid checked the cows at nine p.m. and again at midnight. When he came in, he set the alarm for 2:30, and then fell back on the soft mattress, wondering if he should call Kaitlin to stand-by. *Better safe than sorry.* He reached for the phone by the bedside and dialed her number.

A sleepy voice that wasn't Kait's answered. "Page, tell Kait to get over here. Two heifers dilated and will probably drop tonight. But it's too soon to tell if there's going to be trouble."

"Uh-huh," she moaned.

"Now Page!" he ordered

An hour later, in the midst of light snowfall and twinkling stars, the two women trudged to the barn. Passing the stalls with horses, they spotted Quaid in the last stall. Kaitlin hurried to assist Quaid while Page leisurely looked at the four-five cows in stalls, their swollen bellies alike, and wondered which ones would have babies tonight.

"Over here," Quaid hollered. "Damn, I was afraid of this. She started showing distress about a half hour ago; the calf is breech. I can feel the legs. We'll have to pull 'er." Quaid had a lantern hanging over a stall where a wild-eyed heifer was bellowing in pain. "Stay with her while I get the calf puller."

"I see the hooves. Hurry, Quaid."

He ran to the wall in the barn and yanked off a contraption that looked like looped chain on the end of a stick. He dunked the chain down in a barrel of smelly liquid. Bringing it up dripping, he dunked his hands likewise for sanitary reasons. Opening up the mama wide enough to loop the chain around the calf's legs, he tightened the loop, and then waited for a contraction. Suddenly the mama had a violent contraction at the same time they pulled and a slurpy, sloshy calf slid out.

"Towels!" Kait hollered.

"Where?" Page asked, her eyes darting around.

"In the wooden box behind you. Quick! Hurry!"

Page ran and gathered an armful and hurried over to the newborn calf. Dropping them, she stood watching as Quaid and Kaitlin rubbed the calf briskly and iodined its navel. The baby snorted a plug of mucus before struggling to its feet.

"Watch out, Page," Quaid said, releasing the mother. The heifer sauntered over to her calf to finish licking him off. At that moment, the barn seemed warm and alive.

"Whew! That was a workout." Quaid wiped the sweat off his face with an arm wet with birthing fluids. "Let me wash up and then we'll check #37."

Kaitlin came over to where Page was standing. "And that is how to birth a calf that's in trouble. Thanks for helping."

"But I didn't do anything," Page answered. Fascinated by the birth process, she hoped she would be around for another, although watching them loop the calve puller on the baby's leg and winching it out looked torturous. Apparently, the mother hadn't minded. Busy licking off her calf, mother and son bonded, as Page looked on.

"Hey, I can't be in two places at one time. And that little bull could've frozen to death if I'd left it to go hunt down the towels. The first few minutes are crucial. Let's go inside. Quaid will see that mother and son stay in the barn protected from this frigid air."

The girls stayed the rest of the night filling up on coffee to stay awake. However, the other heifer delivered normally just as dawn was breaking. Afterwards, the three dragged into the house where Kait opened a roll of cinnamon biscuits and popped them in the oven while Page made fresh coffee. Quaid went in the bedroom and collapsed on the bed.

"That was exciting," Page said to Kait

"It gets plenty exciting when you know that calf can die if you don't get it out in time."

"Could I do it next time?" Page asked.

Page had such a look of eagerness on her face Kaitlin didn't want to disappoint her. "Maybe."

Several minutes of silence filled the kitchen before Page broke in: "Is Quaid angry with me? I haven't heard from him since you were in the hospital. I was so surprised to see him at Barnabys. You said he didn't date."

Kait sighed. "I confess. I sent him there. I thought the two of you might have a good time. It is a single's group. And Lord knows he's been single for a long time. But I didn't know he had a date."

"Well, I didn't see him with a date. You? Matchmaking? It doesn't fit you. You knew I was going with Jake."

"It's a free country. A dance don't hurt. You and Jake aren't serious, are you?"

"Well, no, but. . . I suppose Quaid told you what happened. Kait, I just got so nervous and upset. . the two of them vying over me. . . I don't even remember what happened. One minute they were both pulling on me and the next—" She feigned fainting. "Besides, the way I fumbled around on the dance floor, I'd think Quaid would be glad to be rid of me. It was so embarrassing." Page fidgeted with the paper napkin, sopping up coffee drips. "There's something about him I like. But he's never going to let me get close enough to him to know if I could actually care. Maybe I should just give up." As soon as she'd said it, she knew she was lying. It was like a kid wanting candy. The more mother said no, the more the kid wanted it.

121

Kaitlin looked up, "That's funny. He says the same thing about you." Then started singing Mama Don't let Your Babies Grow up to be Cowboys.

CHAPTER TWELVE

Days flowed into weeks as Page dated Jake, enjoying the exposure to different activities. He was a nice man. Always courteous, even chivalrous. Easy to talk with, he never put her down for her naiveté nor criticized her. However, she didn't feel any physical attraction to him. The times she allowed him to kiss her goodnight she felt nothing, feeling guilty returning the slightest affection.

Most of the other members had paired up with each other, which didn't allow for fraternizing, and she considered dropping out of the singles group. Finding a nice man at church didn't seem to be working. Admittedly, she had fun going snowmobiling and cross-country skiing, even welcoming the casual friendship and the resulting fun; the Brulé concert they had attended fostered an intense interest in her for the Sioux Indians. Nevertheless, she felt like she was using Jake. But would Jake be hurt if she told him she didn't want to see him anymore? He was calling every day just to see how she was and what she might be doing and it was beginning to feel cloying. In fact, she was becoming annoyed with it.

If only if it were Quaid. Yet he seemed tied to the ranch 24-7, oblivious to her. If this was his idea of friendship, it sure wasn't close. Rather, she felt like a team player on the bench, only pitching in whenever allowed. Apparently, their tumble on the floor meant nothing. Just more playful teasing. What had he said? He didn't want it to go too far. Hot-cold, sweet-sour, what kind of game was he playing?

*   *   *   *

Rivulets of runoff gushed down the hills and plateaus as the frigid temperatures lessened and the snow melted. The warmer weather stirred a restlessness in Page making her want to be outdoors. A little sad that calving was over, she had enjoyed every minute of it in spite of the fact Quaid wouldn't let her take an active role. He had allowed her to massage and dry the newborns though which gave her much joy.

Guilt ridden at using Jake and still pining for Quaid, she stopped attending the single's group. Jake's calls seemed to drop off thereafter until one day she point blank told him they could never be more than friends, she was pursuing new goals. Afterwards, she wondered where the courage to be so frank came from. Was she changing without even being aware of it?

Sunshine days, cool nights, and halcyon breezes made May heavenly. Page arrived home one day to find a note on the kitchen table. Round-up at Quaid's. Page had run across the word in her novels, but had no idea what it entailed. She would ask Kait when she arrived home.

At eleven p.m. Page called the ranch.

Quaid answered. "We're busy with round-up. Kait's staying here 'til we're through."

"What's round-up?" She toyed in her mind whether to offer a helping hand.

"Rounding up dogies, that's cattle for you city slickers. Branding. Tagging. Castrating. Moving them from one pasture to another."

Page was anxious to see one. She wondered what he would say if she offered to help. Lately, she'd been toying with the idea if Mohammed wouldn't come to the mountain, the mountain would go to Mohammed. If she made herself indispensable . . .

"How about I come out tomorrow? It's Saturday and I could help," she offered.

"I guess you could rustle up some chow while we're working."

Page grimaced. Was that all she was good for—just cooking? "I'll be out right after breakfast."

The next day she crossed through the Double K crossbar, rumbled over the cattle guard, up the twisted lane to the ranch house. Parking the car near the house, she got out and hustled up the back steps into the house, hollering, "Kait! Quaid! I'm here." The house returned silence.

Going back outdoors, a billowing cloud of dust arose near one of the corrals. She stopped short at the sight of several cowboys mounted on horses heading out to the surrounding hills and pastures. Off to her left in a large corral, raucous bleating and bellowing reached her ears. Walking over to the fence, she saw cowboys roping calves, dragging them through the dirt to where Quaid hunkered down over a fire with a red-hot branding iron in his hand. As the Double K brand burned through hair and flesh, she scrunched up her nose, the stench bringing her stomach contents into her throat. As if that weren't bad enough, the cowboys threw the little bulls to the ground and quickly castrated them, throwing their testicles in a pail.

In the midst of all the commotion, she discovered Kaitlin stapling ear tags in branded cattle. The bleating and bellowing bruised her tender heart while the dirt clogged her nostrils making her cough and sneeze. After several

125

minutes, a group of cows ran into another corral. Kaitlin walked over, brushing sweat and dirt from her stained face.

"What'd'ya need, Page?" Kait asked.

"I'm here to help," she said, wondering what she had done to deserve such abruptness.

"Can't talk much now. Guys will be bringing in more doggies. Ask Quaid when he rides in," she said, brushing off her clothes although they would be dirty again within minutes.

"All he said was I could cook," Page answered disappointedly.

"That would be great. We've got about six in the fields roundin' up the cattle and there's. . ." She looked around counting bodies in the corral. "Six here. That's twelve hungry people. Double the helpings. Can you cook for 24? Check out the freezer and cupboards, if there's something you need, just go to the store and charge it to Quaid. Ring the dinner bell up by the porch when it's all ready."

"But, I thought I could do something out here."

"You don't know how important the camp cook is," replied Kait, "You'll be very appreciated by one and all."

Disappointed to be out of the action, Page acquiesced. One meal for twenty-four folks was a tall order, but she could do it. It was better than spending the day alone in Aladdin. It was early enough in the day she had plenty of time to plan, cook, and be ready by twelve-thirty, one o'clock.

Around one-thirty, six hungry, dirty, sweat stained, stinking cowboys came to the back door; Page wondered where she would seat them all.

"Dish it up, we'll eat out here," Quaid said.

Busy as a soup kitchen, in minutes, plates of hamburgers, chips, baked beans, potato salad, taco salad, cookies, and gallons of iced tea and lemonade passed out of her hands. Just as she thought she could take a break to sit down, the next group lined up.

Although she had balked about being cook, she found the cowboys' words gracious and appreciative: "Best damn potato salad I've et for a long time." "What'd she put in these burgers? Damn, they're good. If I wasn't so full, I'd eat me another two, three." "Wish I had me a handful of these cookies out on the range." And the polite, "Thanks ma'am," filled her heart and put a smile on her face.

"Whew! I didn't realize what a job this would be," she said as Kaitlin came up to the door.

"Thank goodness it's only for a couple of weeks," Kaitlin said.

"A couple of weeks! Quaid doesn't own that many cattle, does he? You mean, you're going to do this every day?"

"Yep. I mean, no not here. We ought to be done here this afternoon. When they need us, we'll go help Joe, Riley, Cord, or whoever else needs help. Remember Quaid telling you how we all kind of pitch in together to help one another out?"

Page remembered. There was little she didn't remember when Quaid gave her the time of day. Every word he spoke, every instruction, every gesture was taken in. She craved his conversation like a drink of cool water.

"Who cooks all that time?" she asked, scraping garbage into a large trashcan.

"The ranch wives." Kait bit into the burger, chewing it slowly, savoring the taste.

"Oh," she said, discouraged. "So, I guess after I clean things up, I'm done here, huh?"

"You can stick around for supper. I'm sure one of us could use a backrub."

That evening Page seared T-bones and baked potatoes. After supper, Kait took a shower while Quaid helped clear the table, awaiting his turn to wash up. Page noticed how stiffly he rose from the table. "I could give you a backrub."

He groaned. "I could sure use one. Hey, I forgot to mention, that was a mighty fine feed you provided, I'm obliged."

What is this? Gratitude? "I'm afraid I used up most of your groceries plus what I bought."

"That's all right. Thanks for doin' that."

Where is all this gratitude and politeness coming from?

Just about that time, Kaitlin came out wearing flannel pajamas, rubbing a towel through her dark wet hair. "Your turn, bro."

"I'm pooped," she said to Page who was wiping off the counter.

"Backrub, Madame?" Page enticed her by holding up her hands, spreading and wiggling her fingers.

"Maybe just my neck," she said, rolling it from side to side With her hands she threw her wet hair to the front of her shoulders. She plopped down in a kitchen chair.
Page took the liniment Kait had brought with her, spread some on her hands, and began massaging Kait's neck and shoulder area. Page could feel the tense, taut muscles relax under her squeezing manipulation.

"Give you an hour to quit that." Kait slumped in the chair, thoroughly enjoying the attention.

Warmed with the appreciation, Page continued to massage her until Quaid stepped back into the kitchen.

"My turn," he said, taking Kaitlin's chair while she retired to the living room.

Page took a deep breath at seeing his bare chest with the rippling abs, his large biceps, and the tight smoothness of his back. She began high up on his neck, reaching outward on his tight, tense shoulder muscles. Squeezing his scapular muscles, she caught him flinching. "Too hard?"

"Nah, just hurts right there." He moaned. "I'll give you all night to quit that."

Page giggled. "Your sister said the same thing."

Engrossed in the massage, she wasn't expecting what happened next. He reached up taking her hands, pulling them over his shoulders to his chest. The act pulled Page tautly against his backside, her breasts flattening across his upper back, her head in close proximity to his ears. Fleetingly, she wondered what his sister would think if she walked in as she tried to pull away, but he held her fast. Turning his head upward to the side, he whispered, "Come sit on my lap." Still holding her hands, he maneuvered her around until she stood before him; he pulled her down onto his clean, oatmeal colored, long johns. "Ummm, you still smell like chocolate chip cookies," he said, nuzzling her neck.

She wanted to say she doubted that after her long hours in the kitchen, but she let it pass. His hands stroked her arms; then dropped to her thighs. She tensed. What was happening? What had spawned the amorous feeling in him? Should she respond to the sweeping warmth coming over her?

Before she could say or do anything, he cupped her face in his hands, pulled her close to him and kissed her sweetly. His lips traveled around to her ears. Her little giggle turned into a pleasant moan as he traveled down her neck. As he found her mouth again their breaths quickened. His mouth became more demanding. Moving her hands to cradle his neck, she pulled him closer, wanting him, wanting him to want her. She could feel his erection getting hard as she changed her position to straddle him. He caressed her breasts until the nipples were taut and swollen, confined by the soft brassiere she wore, begging for release. Her head swam with pleasure, her thoughts darting between consensual sex play and stopping him abruptly.

She felt her shirt come out from her jeans. His hands slid up her torso caressing every inch of her flesh. They found purchase on her rising and falling breasts. She breathed heavily, her heart pounding, mind reeling . . . at that moment nothing mattered. His rough chafed hands fumbled at her bra clasp. Unexpectedly, she felt it give way. She felt him rise from the chair and without losing contact with her, carried her into the bedroom, closing the door with a brush from his foot.

As he laid her gently on the bed, she saw the lust in his eyes. Something snapped inside her. What was she doing? She couldn't do this. *You dirty whore.* Michael's voice taunted.

No, no. I'm. . . oh god, that feels soooo good. She felt Quaid's mouth on hers. Kissing her eyes, her nose, her chin, her throat. It had been almost two years since she'd had sex. Would he be gentle? She felt his hands unbuttoning her shirt. She felt him hovering over her, leaning down, kissing her cleavage.

Instantly, as if a bucket of cold water landed on her, her body tightened. She pushed him away. Rolling away from him, tears sprang to her eyes. "I can't, I can't." She rose from the bed pulling her shirt closed. As she looked up to say, "I'm sorry" his cold, hard eyes stared at her. His piercing brown eyes frightened her. What would he do? Would he grab her, hit her, force her to submit as Michael had done? If only she could explain to Quaid. Sensing Quaid's anger at the rejection, she wondered if Michael was right: was she a tease? *Oh, God, how could I let myself get into this situation?* She ran down the hall and out the door.

CHAPTER THIRTEEN

What just happened? What did I do? Quaid followed on her heels, coming out of the bedroom expecting to find her in the house. He checked the other bedroom, the kitchen, the bath, and the living room where Kaitlin lay curled up, fetal style, sound asleep on the couch. Seeing the door open, he rushed over to it. Looking out the screen, he could just make out the taillights at the end of the drive. Damn! He'd messed up again.

He looked over at Kaitlin, dead to the world; he grabbed a blanket and laid it over her. She was a good sister. Many an evening, she had provided a listening ear when he had been going through his divorce with Denise. *I wish she were awake, maybe she could explain Page's erratic behavior.*

He ambled to the kitchen to scour the refrigerator and cupboards for a snack. Page had used all the groceries. He found a dried up slice of baloney and made a sandwich; while he gnawed at it thoughts of Page gnawed in his head.

"What's wrong, Quaid?" Kait asked, stretching and yawning as she stumbled into the kitchen. "Where's Page?"

"Went home, I guess."

"Home? Why? She loves it here." She stretched again. "Mmm, she's good with her hands. That massage put me right to sleep. Is it late?"

"No, you only dozed off for an hour. Hey sis, what's with her? I can't figure her out."

"Um, what's to figure?" Kait said sleepily, while raiding cupboards. Finding a hard gingersnap that had fallen out of the package since who knows when, she broke it in half offering the other half to her brother. "She's crazy about you."

"I don't think so. What do you know about her?"

"Little brother, what do you know about her?"

Stymied, he realized he knew nothing about her, that he hadn't really tried to have any kind of friendship or relationship with her, yet he had been ready to make love to her tonight. "I didn't want to be nosy."

"Maybe you carry that too far. It wouldn't be the first time someone's thought you cold and aloof."

"I'm not cold and aloof. I just mind my own business."

"I see those cogs turning. Just be gentle, Quaid. Her ex was a controller, maybe even violent. I don't know. There's a lot she doesn't say. She did tell me she left Illinois right after the divorce. . . I don't think she has much confidence in herself. She talks about freedom and being self-reliant like the old mountain men. She's way too fragile for that, but I think she's got some hidden strength. She just needs to find her confidence. . . Haven't you noticed how your sharp remarks affect her? It's almost like slapping her in the face. I know you're not one to treat anybody with kid gloves, but maybe you could stop and think before you say things to her." She finished off the cookie before shuffling off to the bedroom.

Sharp remarks?

"Abused? How?" he called after her. He sat up straighter incensed that anyone would abuse a woman.

"I've probably said too much as it is. Why don't you ask her? Goodnight," she called back.

Divorced. How well he knew that pain. That sense of failure. That struggle to start over. But abused? What made Kait think she'd been abused? How? Physically? Mentally? Both? The words sloshed around in his head. He wondered if the pain she felt was anything like the pain he'd felt with Denise. And what had he done? Stayed his distance. Been critical. Shut her out. Made fun of her. What had she ever done to him?

Tonight, rubbing his shoulders, he just naturally assumed it was foreplay. Her coming on to him. Maybe she hadn't meant it to be that way at all. Was she wrestling with her feelings as well? Maybe he needed a different approach. Abused animals needed TLC. Maybe that's what Page Chandling needed. And a big apology.

Unexpectedly a rush of anger flooded over him. Anger at her ex. Anger at his ex. Anger at all the spouses in the world who mistreated one another. He walked over to a cabinet in a corner of the kitchen. Drawing out a bottle of Jack Daniels he poured himself a shot, swallowed it in one gulp, poured another for good measure and sat there mulling over the situation.

Page could barely concentrate on her driving as she thought about what just happened. Meaning only to help ease the day's aches and pains, she hadn't read anything into giving him a massage. Yet he had responded in a way she wasn't expecting. She knew all about physical attraction. She'd had lust with Michael. Now she wanted something more—something different. She craved intimacy without sex; she wanted, needed, trust, friendship, loyalty, respect, kindness. Was that possible with a man or did they all have their heads between their legs? Although she was hungry to be close to him, hungry for his touch, she hadn't expected anything sexual. Not now, not so soon. Yet, she had probably encouraged him by sitting on his lap, by allowing him to explore her body. Oh God! She was everything Michael said she was—a cheap slut.

That night, Page tossed and turned berating herself with recriminations.

Tired and restless, after breakfast the next morning, she decided a walk might do her good. She followed the road for a distance, the warm mid-morning sun striking her back, forcing her to shed her jacket. A mountain peak rose in the distance. Setting it as her goal, she headed in its direction. Huffing and puffing, she discovered what might be a shortcut—a break in a fence line where a vehicle could drive through—and followed it.

Unaware where she placed her feet, unexpectedly, one of her feet started sinking. As she tried to pull it out, the mud clung tenaciously weighing her boot down. It felt like a ton. The more she pulled, the more it sucked and her foot sunk deeper and deeper. Attempting to free herself, soon the other foot sunk in the sticky clay like substance. Arms flailing, she tumbled backwards just as a gravelly voice said, "Hey what do you think you're doing? "

She looked up to see a man sucking on a cigarette, aiming a rifle at her.

Frightened, she said, "D-don't shoot. I was just out walking. I'm stuck. "

He shook his head. "You're not from around here are you? "

She shook her head, her blonde hair floating through the air.

"Didn't think so. You're trespassing."

"I didn't see a sign, " she grunted, struggling to get out of the muck.

"Don't need one. You don't go on other people's land without asking. Got that? We don't take lightly to trespassing. You'll get yourself killed."

Taken aback, she asked, "Just for walking? "

"You betcha. Us ranchers aren't going to be liable for accidents on our land. And stay out of the gumbo." He laid the rifle aside and stretched out his hand. In one quick jerk he pulled her upright.

Gumbo? The only gumbo Page knew about was Louisiana gumbo, a chowder type soup. This was gumbo? She had read about the alkali out here, clay soil with a high sodium percentage. If you looked at the land, you could actually see where the white chalkiness covered the poor soil like salt, the areas often wet from low infiltration.

"I'm sorry sir. It won't happen again," she said turning to go.

"See to it it doesn't." He stood watching her until she met the road.

Embarrassed, she dragged herself back to the road where the drying mud was tightening her clothes into Frankenstein stiffness. Rudely awakened that her walk had come to such an abrupt end, she wondered just where she could wander. For all that hype about wide-open spaces, it seemed the ranchers had a special market on it. Most all the rural land had fences around it. Where was the Wyoming of her westerns? The wide-open spaces? It sure wasn't like she had imagined. She thought she could go anywhere.

Five days passed. While Kaitlin and Quaid went from ranch to ranch helping with round-up, Page tried to rationalize the reasons Quaid hadn't called her recently. Did he think she was still seeing Jake Stoner? She understood now how a rancher had to be around during calving; she understood round-up. She liked the fact that everyone pitched in to help someone else out. That would explain his busyness. Or was it that she hadn't given herself over to him the other night? She'd been so terrified at giving herself so freely, all she could think of was getting as far away as possible, as quickly as possible.

Page busied herself with Kait's chores, and caring for Brandy, Kait's horse. Other times, she amused herself by going out to a landfill to practice her shooting skills. Kait had shown her the basics and she had purchased a second hand .38 caliber revolver from a pawnshop. At first, it made her nervous handling a weapon; the loud retort was much more deafening than she ever imagined. After a while, she enjoyed the challenge of trying to hit tin cans, yet seeing the large exit holes the bullets made, she hoped she would never have to pull the trigger on a helpless animal, predator or no. She laughed. That wasn't the kind of thinking a mountain man would take. She'd been foolish to think she was going to be another Grizzly Adams. Instantaneously, an analogy came to mind: Predator-Michael. Would she have to use her revolver against him one day?

The following day Kaitlin returned to hear Page break the news she was moving on. It was time to decline any more of the Kincaid's hospitality. They had kept her all winter. She had a fair amount of money saved and it was time to strike out on her own.

Just as Page was breaking the news, the phone rang. "Hello?" she said.

"Page? I, uh, was wondering if you'd like to go out for dinner tonight. Branding's done and. . . . "

Quaid's slow, easy drawl made her heart beat so fast she thought it would burst. She didn't think she'd ever hear his voice again.

"Are you sure that's what you want to do?" she asked. "I wasn't very nice to you the last time we were together."

"I'm sure."

"Yes, I'd like that very much."

"Page? I'm sorry about what happened when you were here." There was silence on the line. "I was out of line."

Had she heard right? Quaid Kincaid apologizing? Even his voice seemed different. Unsure what to say, she mumbled, "Me too." Hanging up the phone, she broke out in a big grin. *He can't think I'm bad, or a tease, or any of the nasty things Michael called me. Oh happy day! He's giving me another chance.*

* * * *

Alone in the dark movie theater, Page hoped Quaid would put his arm around her, maybe whisper in her ear about the movie or something. She wanted to snuggle up to him. Instead, he sat eating his popcorn, hunched down in the seat, intensely engrossed in the picture. As they left the theater, Page asked, "Do you think we could go back to that little drive-in café that has buffalo burgers?"

"You still hungry?" he asked, amazed where she could put it after a dinner of prime rib, baked potatoes, salad and pecan pie.

"Not really. Maybe a malted or something to drink. I just don't want tonight to end."

Parked curbside at the Whitehorse, the girl brought their drinks. They sipped them quietly for a moment, before Page opened the conversation. "Quaid, why did you take me out tonight? Did Kait put you up to it? What is it about me that you don't like?"

He startled. "What makes you think I don't like you?"

"Well, you haven't exactly made me feel welcome. You didn't want me around during calving. You seemed angry when I went to the dance with Jake. You relegated me to the kitchen for round-up. You haven't called for days. On the other hand, you tried to get me to bed. I don't understand you."

"Understand me," he muttered. "Understand *me*? What about *you*—" He caught himself before things turned into senseless arguing. He twisted in the seat to face her.

"I like you. It's just that. . . I dunno, you're a city girl. City ways. I guess maybe I haven't been fair with you. Look, I've been married before. I got taken to the cleaners. I haven't got anything to offer you." It was the brutal truth.

Every ounce of her being was screaming, *yes, yes you do have something to offer me,* but she couldn't say that aloud.

"I've been married too, Quaid. And. . . . Michael wasn't. . . very nice. . . to me."

"Kait said you've been abused." He brushed the hair away from her eyes so he could see their expression.

"W-What?" She swatted his hand away and looked him straight in the face. "Kait told you? How could she? I told her in confidence. What else did she tell you?"

"Just that she thought you'd been abused. And that I was being too rough on you."

"So now you feel sorry for me. I see what this date is all about." Her voice rose with ire as she shifted to face forward, her body stiffening, setting her jaw.

"Page, don't do this. Tell me about him. Tell me about Michael. What he did to you," he coaxed. He slid his arm around her shoulder, but she jerked it away. He ran his hand over her hair, down her neck, massaging the growing tension.

"How about you tell me about Denise?" she spat.

Recoiling, he dropped his hand from her neck and jerked back into the driver's seat turning sour. How did she know about Denise? It had to be Kaitlin. What right did she have to mention Denise to Page? He'd' have to have a talk with Kaitlin. Right now he and Page needed to talk, but could he confide in a woman he barely knew?

"Remember when I told you I didn't have anything to offer you? That's because Denise drained me dry in the divorce. I had to file bankruptcy. If Denise had helped me, I'd have a bigger spread, more cattle, even a better house. You probably think I'm some big time rancher. I'm not. I've worked my tail off just to keep the land I inherited. Come close to losin' it all more than once. Had to build the herd up one by one. As it is, all I've got is a few head of cattle and debt over my head. Seems like every step forward, I get put back two . . . have to sell off a cow or steer before I can raise replacements. I ain't got no money, no way of supporting a wife. And you know I depend on Kait for a lot of stuff.

"I hurt real bad when Denise cheated on me. I thought we were going to make a go of things." Pain etched his face at the recollection. He firmed his jaw and looked out the window, unsure he wanted to continue. After several seconds, he continued, "Thought we wanted the same things. She finally showed her true colors."

A wife? Was he aware of what he'd just said? Was he thinking of supporting a wife? Who? She decided to let the remark slip. "I'm sorry you were hurt so bad." She gently laid her hand on his arm in sympathy. "I guess some people hold grudges, others have a chip on their shoulder, and others can shake things off and start new." Her words came out smooth as molasses, yet unsure how much to divulge, she continued, "I don't know what Kaitlin told you, but when I met Michael, he made me feel like a movie star, really special, you know? I fell hard and after we married, he started acting crazy—telling me where I could go, only giving me ten minutes to get home from the store, and if I wasn't, he would accuse me of being with someone else. He even told me what I had to wear each day."

"That must have been hard on you, being pinned to the wall like that. You should have left him. Wasn't there anyone you could talk to, get some help?"

She shook her head. "I wasn't supposed to have any friends. I guess he saw that as some kind of threat, even though I don't understand it. Leave? I was too afraid to leave. Help? Like what, a shrink? That would have gone over like a lead weight. No, he had me where he wanted me. He started running around on me. Of course, it was okay for him. Double standards, you know."

He hesitated. "Did he ever hit you?" The thought of her ex striking her sent an arrow of pain through him.

A tear trickled down her cheek. "More than I want to recall. But that wasn't the worst."

"I don't know if I want to hear this, but go on." He clenched his teeth apprehensive yet growing angrier by the minute.

"I'm afraid of him. Before the divorce, he hit me with a shotgun and broke my jaw."

Full of contempt, he spat, "Scumbag—I hate men that abuse women. And you divorced him, right?"

"I don't know how to say this." She looked in her lap. "I feel so stupid."

"You're not stupid, Page." He reached over and took hold of her hand hoping it would convey assurance.

She began weeping. "It was the final straw for me, but I felt guilty. I thought I still loved him. I didn't know how I was going to see an attorney when he kept such close tabs on me. He canceled his earlier filing. Tried to make out how sorry he was. I should have let him go ahead with it. It was only because I countersued that he hit me. After that, I had to have reconstructive surgery. During that time, with the help of my doctor, I found the strength to divorce him. But it was nasty. I thought it would all be over, but as I left the courtroom, he told me, 'You'll never be out of my sight, never out of my life.' That's when I decided to move out here."

"What does that mean? He's not here in Wyoming, is he? Has he bothered you?""

"Noooo, at least not yet. But I go around on pins and needles."

"Aw, sounds like bluff. He must have an ego problem. I wouldn't worry about him, Page. How long has it been since your divorce?"

She thought a moment. She had left Leitchfield the end of September. It was almost June. "Eight months."

"Hey, the guy's over you. C'mon now, dry those pretty blue eyes of yours. It's time to start living again."

She heard the words; she just couldn't believe them. Should she tell Quaid how much Michael still mentally influenced her?

A rapping on the window startled them both. Quaid rolled down the window.

"Sorry. We're closing. You'll have to leave the premises." One by one the neon lights went out leaving them in darkness.

CHAPTER FOURTEEN

No doubt as disturbed by her revelations as she was about his life with Denise, Page assumed Quaid would take her home. However, Quaid drove past the city limits of Newcastle. Where were they going? Soon she recognized County Road Seven and knew they were heading for the Double K. Why? What more was there to say? They rode quietly until they arrived at the ranch.

They sat on the lumpy couch for an hour or more talking, each opening up to the other as never before. It pained her to hear Quaid talk about how Denise had cheated on him, afterwards demanding such a costly divorce settlement. No wonder he had to struggle for everything. No wonder he was so bitter. Listening to him describe Denise's actions she knew she was just the opposite. She told him about her life with Michael, how she pinched the grocery budget to get away, how much she still feared Michael, how she came to realize her wannabe mountain man dreams had been just that and she was grounding herself in reality now. Still sorting them out herself, the only thing she left out were her true feelings for him. Attracted to him beyond reason since their encounters in the barn and on the butte, she knew she wasn't the kind of woman who could retain hatred towards all men. She certainly didn't hate Quaid; she thought she understood him better after their talk this evening. But was she ready for another relationship?

She watched his face as she told her story. The deep concern and injustice of Michael's abuse shown plainly on it. Had she caused him more anguish telling him?

"Page, Page, I want to take your pain away," he whispered, wrapping his arm around her shoulder, pulling her in close to him. He took hold of her hands, which she'd been wringing in her lap, stroking them gently with his thumbs. His hand moved up her arm, caressing it, until it arrived at her neck. He turned her face towards him and gently kissed her.

The pain she'd been unaware of harboring for so many months welled within her; tears pooled in her eyes and trickled down her face. Feeling his gentle caresses, his kiss, his rough, work hardened hands wiping it away. He kissed her again, this time deeper, longer. Heat rose within her as she returned his kiss.

She felt his warm breath, the wisp of his lips as they played over her eyes, her cheeks, her ears, down her neck. She didn't want him to stop. She felt him slide his arm around her and pull her down with him on the couch. Lying on top of him, she felt his hard, muscled body, and then the growing bulge in his groin. He took her hand and led it to the bulge. She instinctively knew what he wanted.

"I want you, Page. I want you now."

Want. Michael had taught her the difference between need and want. Quaid wanted her. For a split second, she questioned if love had anything to do with his wanting or if it was sex. She had no time to consider.

Consumed by the rising heat in her as he ran his hands up under her shirt and caressed her breasts, he slipped her bra straps off her shoulders, nudging the bra downward to where he could touch and fondle her breasts without its constraint. At that point, she knew she wanted him too. He continued to caress her until both of them were breathing heavily, breathlessly. When he looked in her eyes for approval, she gave it. Scooping her up, he carried her to the bedroom laying her gently on the bed.

"Are you okay with this?" he asked, his voice husky with lust.

She nodded.

"Do you want me to undress you or do you want to?"

"I want to undress you," she said in a voice so full of desire she didn't recognize it as her own.

The morning sun blared through the window warming the room and the bed where Page lay. Baring her soul and last night's lovemaking left her deeply satisfied and relaxed. Quaid had been gentle and slow with her. When he came in her, she was sure she had found her one true love.

She stretched her arm out to touch Quaid only to be alarmed to find the bed empty. She jumped up, wrapping the sheet around her and tore through the small bungalow halting at the kitchen.

"Hey, sleepyhead. Sleep well?" he drawled, over his cowboy coffee.

Taking a deep breath, she beamed. "Like a baby."

"I guess baring our souls helped us both. Thought maybe we'd go riding today. Ever been on a horse?" He took his booted foot and shoved a chair out for her to sit on.

She poured her coffee and sat down, hugging the loose wrapping around her. "Sure."

"Take your time. Drink your coffee. I'll start chores. Besides it will be a little warmer in an hour or two."

She nodded her assent as the screen door banged shut. Still feeling his kisses, a mild case of whisker burn and the lingering musky scent of sex, she wasn't sure she wanted to wash it away in a shower. Reveling in the afterglow of last night's lovemaking, she took this as the sign of a wonderful relationship that could only grow as the days went by. Lengthening the time it took to drink a cup of coffee and chew a piece of toast, a half hour went by before she even thought of showering.

The smell of leather and horse greeted her as she walked into the tack room where Quaid was picking up a saddle. "Get a couple of those blankets, would you?" he motioned with his head to the fence stall. He took the blanket from her, laying it over the horse's back before throwing the saddle over and adjusting the cinch strap. "You ever ride?"

Why is he asking again? Isn't he listening? "Once or twice, years ago. Just a trail ride. One horse following another. Nothing like Roy Rogers or the Lone Ranger," she said, stroking the horse's forehead.

Quaid laughed. "Dating yourself aren't you? I remember watching the re-runs of those ol' Saturday mornin' shoot-em-ups as a kid."

"I always wanted to ride like that," she said wistfully. "The Lone Ranger was my hero."

"Can't. You'll wear a horse out faster than spit. Lope, canter, walk, but a full out run's only good for a few minutes."

"Pooh," she said screwing up her face. "I always thought it would be thrilling to gallop over the plains like in the movies. Why is everything so misleading? Reality sucks."

He shook his head. "Guess that's just life." He walked the pinto mare up beside her and stopped holding the reins out to her.

"Ready? First, you always get on from the left side. Grab the reins, grab the horn, get your left foot in the stirrup, spring yourself up and swing your right leg over." He was standing so close to her she could smell the clean, fresh scent of Irish Spring soap emanating from his morning shower; it was such a turn-on she wished they could go back in the house and repeat last night's lovemaking. Delighted their intimacy had brought them closer, she turned her mind back to the moment; she knew how to mount a horse, but she wasn't going to chance irritating him by cutting his instructions short.

"If she doesn't respond to knee pressure, give her a little kick with your foot if you want her to go faster. Pull the reins whatever way you want her to go. Just don't pull back too fast or too tight or she might rear."

She led her horse out of the barn, jiggling from side to side in the saddle, as she kept in step with Quaid's gelding. When they reached open pasture, he motioned his horse to trot. The pinto she rode followed in pace, and Page felt herself slip and slide in the saddle as she tried to keep her feet in the stirrups. Gripping the horn hard she tried to keep her legs from bouncing. As they bounced inward, it seemed the horse picked up speed. Loping along side by side, unexpectedly the mare took off in a full run.

"WHOAAAAA, WHOAAAAA," Page yelled, drawing back on the reins, while trying to stay seated. Scenery flashed past her quick as lightening.

Out of the corner of her eye, she saw the gelding and the next thing she knew Quaid grabbed the reins and stopped the horse. Page wobbled back and forth as if she might fall off.

"Are you okay? What happened?"

146

Her face flushed, she gasped, "I guess maybe I kicked a little too hard; I don't know it happened so fast."

"Let's rest here a minute before heading up to high country. There's a pretty, little lake up there."

Scaling the hills and valleys on horseback gave her an entirely new perspective on the land—the grasses, the hard pack, the rocky talus. Quaid pointed out different plants, weeds and grasses. She delighted seeing her first mountain bluebird. The higher they climbed the air grew thinner making it more difficult to breathe. At the crest of a butte, Quaid reined up. Page did likewise and was amazed at the sight. The expanse was awesome. She could see for miles and miles. It made her feel small in comparison.

"What'd'ya think?" Quaid pointed to a mountain lake, blue as any picture postcard.

"It's gorgeous. Oh! What was that?" she asked seeing something dark swimming the surface of the water.

"Looks like a muskrat."

A baying echoed the air as they sat their horses looking at the land.

"Is that a wolf?" she asked.

"No, coyotes callin'."

"Umm, I like that. Are they close by?"

"Hard to say. Probably not. Up here you can hear as well as see for miles."

As they moved down country, all of a sudden something flashed by a few feet ahead of them. The pinto danced nervously as Page screamed. Barely catching a glimpse of what it could be, she scanned her neck to see while asking, "What was that?"

"Bobcat. Don't see one too often. They keep to themselves. Hide in the trees most of the time."

"Are there . . . bears . . . up here?" she asked nervously.

"Not in this area. At least none ever reported. You'd have to get into some wilder territory and different elevation."

"Then they do exist out here?"

"Sure. Mountain lions too."

She looked around anxiously keeping a watchful eye out for unseen dangers.

"What's this?" she asked, moseying up to a bush with deep pink, almost fuchsia flowers. "How pretty." Page reached out to grab the branch and raise it to her nose. "Ouch!" She retracted her hand and sucked her finger.

"Those are prairie roses. Thorny. And if you keep sticking your nose in them, you may get stung. Somehow a big schnoz doesn't suit you." He grinned.

She smiled. "I'd love to pick some." She dismounted; her legs like wet noodles. She had to hold on to the horn to keep from crumpling.

"Allow me." He dismounted. Pulling a jackknife from his pant pocket, he cut several blossoms off, despite getting scratched and poked, then hacked away at the thorns. He handed them to her. "Pretty roses for a pretty lady."

"For me?" She blushed. "How chivalrous." Had he changed overnight? This was a side of him she hadn't seen before. This Quaid she liked. But how long would it last? Would he turn into a monster again at any minute? Reaching for the bouquet, she noticed his cut, scratched hands just as he withdrew them, forcing her to reach and step closer to him. Inching closer and closer, she took his teasing good-naturedly. All at once, she lunged for them. When she did, he pulled his hand back over his head and with his other hand drew her in close to him. He quickly kissed her on the cheek before presenting her with the flowers.

"If that's what picking flowers does to you, I'll demand flowers every day," she teased back.

She felt his other arm come around her, pulling her in to him. His eyes caressed her before he leaned in and she felt his warm breath on her face, his lips brushing hers. She closed her eyes enjoying the pleasure spreading through her. Their kisses heating up, they explored each other's mouths with their tongues. The bouquet of flowers slipped from her hand. On fire with passion, they agreed to return to the ranch house, pronto.

They had just broken the rise when the pinto cried out in fright. Page, afraid of falling off, pulled the reins tightly. The horse reared, twisted and turned, raising itself up on its hind legs, pawing the air. Like a shot, the pinto turned and ran full gallop out to the far reaches of a butte. Page held on with all her might frightened by the speed of the animal. Seeing a fence line, Page feared the horse would jump it or get tangled in it and she would surely fall. Could she stop in time? Abruptly, she felt herself airborne. Landing with a thud, she felt the wind knocked out of her and something needlelike pierce her hand. Within seconds, Quaid was beside her feeling her arms and legs.

"You all right?"

But she couldn't breathe.

"I don't feel any broken bones. Can you stand up?"

Blowing out a heavy breath, slightly disoriented, she staggered to her feet with his help. A second later, the jarring fall set in. Sore and bruised, she tried to straighten up. Her hand prickled and stung.

"Rattler spooked her. A little early in the year for 'em but must be the warm sunshine . . . out sunbathin'."

"R-R-Rattlers?" she quivered. "Out here?" Deathly afraid to look at her hand, she imagined any moment she'd feel its poison go through her. So, this is how my life will end. "My hand," she said weakly as the pain increased. "How long . . . have I got?"

He touched her arm and turned her hand over. He laughed. "Well, ma'am, I'd say at least forty, fifty years. But we best get back to the ranch where I can pull those cactus spines out." He whistled and the pinto she had been riding appeared. "Let me give you a hand up. You don't want to drive them thorns in any deeper than they are."

Back at the ranch, he laid tweezers, disinfectant and Bag Balm on the kitchen table. Motioning her into a chair, he sat opposite her. He turned her palm upward and rubbed the underside to soothe her. "I'm not going to tell you this won't hurt a mite."

Taking the tweezers he began extracting the large thorns one by one, concentrating on the task, so he wouldn't see the pain on her delicate face.

"Um, these aren't bad. Seen worse. Many a cowboy's had thorns in 'em. Some in some pretty bad places."

Tears rolling down her creeks, she said, "In case you haven't noticed, I'm not a cowboy." She sniffed.

"Oh, I've noticed. Yes, sirree, I can definitely vouch you are not a cowboy." He determined to keep the mood light.

Wincing each time another spine came out, she watched her hand swell up. "Look at this. Now what am I going to do?" she wailed.

He pulled her hand back towards him to complete the job. Each time he looked up at her face, she feigned stoically how little it hurt.

"That's it. Now come hold your hand out over the sink."

She recognized the orange stuff he was pouring on her hand as the same he'd covered his arms with during calving.

"Disinfectant. Let it dry some. Now, give me your hands."

Dutifully she presented them as he reached in a green tin can, smearing out a glob of thick, petroleum looking gunk. She looked at the can and read aloud, "Bag Balm, for minor cuts and abrasions, cow's teats and udders, etc. You must have grabbed the wrong stuff. This is for cows."

"This here is the best stuff in the world. Wouldn't be a rancher in the valley doesn't swear by Bag Balm. You'll be healed up in no time."

Lulled by his strong hands rubbing and caressing hers, she barely heard what he said. It felt so good she didn't want him to quit.

CHAPTER FIFTEEN

"That was great! Until I fell on the cactus. Can we go riding again tomorrow?" she asked eagerly after the throbbing subsided. Her eyes twinkled like stars dancing with anticipation.

"Enjoyed that, did you? If you're not too stiff and sore. Do you good to take a long soak in the tub, though."

The sexual tension they'd felt on the mountain dissipated with her accident. First aid for her hand overtook any lingering thoughts of replaying last night's lovemaking. Although still sore, the acute pain had left. Jumping up she hustled to the door.

"Hey, where are you going?" he called after her as she went out the door.

"Rub down the horses," she called over her shoulder.

"Turning into a horse woman, are you? What about your hand?" he called out the screen door, grinning.

She hollered back, "You live out here, you're going to have a few aches and pains."

Huh! She had been listening. Minutes later, he stood inside the barn door observing her. He watched as she brushed and rubbed down the horses. He thought about her willingness to come out to the ranch at all hours of the day and night, her willingness to learn, the way her face lit up rubbing down the calves. Although he'd originally figured her for a pansy, here she was giving it her all, despite a swollen hand. Denise would have milked the situation for a week. He had to admit Page had grit. She might become a ranch woman yet.

Seeing her stretch to reach the fourteen hands high gelding, it reminded him of her stretching to get the roses. How her body had. . . . *The roses! She left them on the butte.* At that moment, he resolved to get her more. He also thought about last night's lovemaking—seeing her naked body, how her nipples peaked under his manipulation, hearing her gasps and moans of pleasure as she orgasmed, and waking up with her beside him this morning. Right now, he was ready to resume where they'd left off. He had an idea. He walked over to a flaked hay bale tearing out a handful. He waited until she backed out of the stall. When she tripped on the toe of his boot, she teetered backward and forward, falling into his chest. As she whirled around to face him, he playfully tossed the hay at her.

"Hey! What was that for?" she said putting a hand on her hip, indignant.

"Hay? Yes, I do believe this is hay, ma'am," he said in all seriousness before breaking into a foolish grin. He boot kicked up a clean handful that had fallen out of the stall and started menacingly towards her. His big brown eyes danced mischievously. In a flash, he lurched towards her and in one quick movement stuffed it down the front of her shirt.

Her eyes widened, her mouth opened agape, surprised he would do such a thing.

Determined he wasn't the only the only one who could play games, Page ran to the haystack and grabbed a handful. She turned to toss it at him, but he was standing inches away.

153

"Are you going to throw that at me, lady?" He wrapped his arms around her waist and rocked her.

"No. I'm going to stuff it down your pants," she threatened, her eyes narrowing. Taking her other hand, she pulled the waistline of his jeans away from his body.

"I'll clean you up if you clean me up," he teased, wrestling away before she could do anything.

"Don't tempt me, Kincaid. Now, go on, I've got work to do." Her bravado fading, she turned back to the horse stalls.

"Hold still! Don't move!"

Hearing the alarm in his voice, she froze. "What is it?"

"It. . .looks like. . . a Kincaid spider," he said seriously.

She gave a small shriek, "Get it off me!"

He came up behind her placing his hands on her shoulders, then let his hands drift down over her backside, around the curve of her buttocks, before working his way back up around the sides of her waist, and finally resting on her breasts.

She whirled around. "You! There's no such thing as a Kincaid spider. Except the one feeling me all over." She giggled as he pulled her close. Wrapping her arms around him, she awaited his lips.

CHAPTER SIXTEEN

They made love again and by late afternoon, Page felt sore, both vaginally and in the tightening muscles in her back and sore hand. She just wanted to go to bed— alone, without Quaid. She told him she was heading back to Aladdin and kissed him goodbye. Halfway out the door, the telephone rang.

"I'll get it," Page said.

"Page, I'm so glad you're there." Kaitlin's voice sounded strange, agitated

"What's wrong?"

"Whatever you do, stay there!"

"Okay, but why?" A dread of ominous news plagued her.

"Michael. He's here in Wyoming. He knows you've been living with me. Anyway, he wouldn't tell me what he wanted, but he's determined to find you. You've got to tell Quaid in case he goes out there."

Page's felt the blood drain from her face. Her heart pounded in her chest. Her hands felt cold, yet clammy. Her mouth went dry. *Michael. In Wyoming. After all these months, why?* She knew Michael would stop at nothing to get what he wanted. He could talk a good game and get information out of just about anyone.

"Y-You mean he came to the house?"

"No, but he did say he was in Wyoming. It may have been a cell call. It kept breaking up."

"What else did he say?"

"Nothing much, just that he's determined to find you. If he's as dangerous as you say, you had better stay there. And tell Quaid now, or I will. I see what you mean about being a real charmer. I thought it was somebody from the singles group or somebody at work. He just asked for you. How was I to know it was Michael? I said you weren't here. In an instant, he sounded driven and angry. I'm sorry, Page. I just didn't know it was him."

Snapping out of her stupor, Page said, "I hope he didn't do anything to you, did he? I mean, he didn't threaten you or anything, did he?"

"No. I'm all right. But be sure you tell Quaid."

Page stood still as the phone went dead. Hands shaking, she hung up on her end and looked at Quaid.

"What is it?" he asked observing her alarm and distress. "What's wrong?" He grabbed her shoulders, gently shaking her. "Answer me, damn it!"

The shaking brought her out of her hypnotic trance. Her eyes fluttered, grew wide with shock, her lips quivered and she bit down on them to stem the fear overtaking her. In a whisper she said, "Oh God, its Michael."

Quaid studied her. "What about Michael?" he asked sternly.

"He-He's here. He's found me." At that moment every wonderful thing that had happened in the past few months, every friend she had made, everything she had learned, and everyplace she had gone, turned sour. Tormenting thoughts fled through her. Had he been watching her? Did he put a detective on her trail? Were her friends going to be in danger now? Her old feelings of being captive foamed. "Oh God, what am I going to do?" she whispered, closing her eyes, wishing it would all go away.

"That was Michael on the phone? How did he get my number?"

"No, no. That was Kaitlin. Somehow, he located her. Someone must have seen us together. I dunno." Agitated, she continued, "He has ways. . . He must have thought I'd be there. I wish I was. No, no, I don't mean that. Well, maybe. If I were there, I wouldn't have to worry about him finding you. Us. About finding me here with you. He'll kill you if he doesn't kill me first. He could be violent."

"I don't get it. Why would he come after you after all this time? Is he still in love with you?"

"Love me? I dunno. Maybe in his warped way. I've got to get out of here," she said, anxiously looking around for a way to escape.

"No. You're staying put. He doesn't know where you are. You're safe here." He walked over to where she stood and wrapped his arms around her protectively.

Pushing him away, she said, "You don't know Michael, Quaid. If he could hunt down Kaitlin, he'll find you too." Her voice rose in panic as she trembled. Fear flushed her face.

"Is he really that bad? Maybe we should see what Michael wants before you get all upset."

"Whatever it is, it can't be good. What if he hurts you or Kaitlin? I couldn't bare that. You've both been so kind to me."

He reached out and lifted up her chin, cupping her cheek, his thumb gently caressed her cheek. "Look at me, Page." He gathered her trembling hands in his. "I can handle myself. And I won't let anything happen to you either. I love you." He leaned in and kissed her tenderly.

He loves me, he loves me! Not once during their lovemaking had he said he loved her. Why now? Did he realize what he had just said? It was too soon to be the real thing, wasn't it? Her heart turned cartwheels at the

157

proclamation. She snuggled into his embrace feeling his strong arms hold her gently, his strength comforting her, giving her the security she needed at that moment. Did he mean it the way she wanted him to or was it just his way of comforting her?

"I love you too." The words glided off her tongue. No sooner had they slipped out than it dawned on her something had happened to both of them. They were coming together as one.

She broke away. Pacing nervously from window to window, she kept looking out at the long drive, expecting Michael to show at any moment, yet praying he wouldn't. The wind in the trees danced shadows over the yard alarming her, making her think she saw someone running, hiding behind the barn, by the corral,. behind her car. Every rustle, every sound set her on edge. Every whinny from the horses made her whirl around in panic

She looked over at Quaid, standing helpless, wondering what to do. He said he'd keep her safe. How she wanted to let him, but if she did, didn't that make her a coward? Shouldn't she stand up to Michael? She hadn't changed a bit. Still afraid of Michael she was cowering behind Quaid. Yet if she did stand up to her ex, would she live to see Quaid another day?

Quaid stood helpless watching the fear rise in Page. *Was Michael as dangerous as Page said? What could he want?* He never understood why some men felt they had to beat their spouse into submission. Spouse. She wasn't even his spouse anymore. In any case, he'd see to it Michael didn't hurt Page. She'd been through enough hell. A twinge of guilt swept over him as he recalled how he had probably contributed to it. Ashamed of his sarcasm and shortness with her, he wished he could retract and replay those earlier days. He determined to never hurt her or be cruel to her again. He loved her. As if being thunked by a fly ball, he realized what he'd just said. Assimilating it, within seconds, he accepted it. He loved Page Chandling.

A dark rain cloud scudded through his mind. *Is that why Michael's here? Did he realize his mistake in divorcing Page? Does he still love her? Is he here to take her away?* He couldn't let that happen.

Headlights! From a distance, Page could not tell who it was. Had Michael found her? She ran into the bedroom shutting the door behind her. Heart pumping, adrenalin racing, she peeked around the window shade. *Michael wouldn't lower himself to a truck, would he? But if he was trying to surprise me, catch me off guard...*

Kaitlin stormed into the house yelling their names.

"What? What is it?" Page asked with urgency as she walked into the room, relieved it was Kaitlin who'd arrived in the old Ford.

"Why didn't you answer the phone? I've been calling and calling."

"I'm sorry, Kait. I was afraid it might be Michael. I left it off the hook."

"Where's Quaid? Did you tell him?" Kait looked sternly at her. Page nodded her head. "I dunno. He was here a few minutes ago. But when I saw you come up the drive, I thought it might be Michael and I went and hid in the bedroom."

Kait went flying down the hall. Not finding Quaid anywhere in the house she ran towards the barn.

Page followed.

"Quaid! I think Michael's followed me here. I thought I could lose him, but he's been behind me most of the way. If I did lose him, he's smart. He'll ask around until he finds us. He's looking for Page," she said breathlessly.

He dropped the tack he was oiling to walk up to the house, the girls at his heels. He reached into a corner of the mudroom and brought out a .30-.30 lever action rifle.

159

Page gasped. "Is that necessary?" she asked, bug-eyed.

"If he's as violent as you say, yes. No s.o.b. is gonna mess with us."

"Oh no! Here comes another car," Page cried, as a flash of bright lights reflected in the afternoon sun. All the old feelings of terror returned as she anticipated Michael's visit.

"Get in the house," Quaid ordered.

Once inside, Page tried hiding in a couple of places, but Kaitlin pulled her out saying, "No hiding. Face the enemy. Let him see you're not afraid of him."

"But I am!" she wailed.

"Still, you're not going to let him know it. You've done nothing wrong. You have every right to be here, to have the life you want. Let him see he can't bully you anymore."

Quaid planted himself on the opposite side of the doorframe, out of sight. When a raucous pounding and shouting started, he motioned for Page to answer the door. She shook her head. Kaitlin gave her a push. Quaking, she slowly pulled the door open and faced her ex through the screen door.

"Michael?" her voice quivered. "Michael, is that you? The man standing at the door was a shadow of the man she had been married to. His jet-black hair had turned gray and thin. His $800 suit hung on a skeletal frame. His California tan was a pasty gray. What had happened to him? He had once been so handsome; now he looked worn and beaten down.

"So it's true. I've found you. Aren't you going to let me in?"

His voice was still strong and proud. Afraid to let him in for fear he would not leave or would forcefully take her, she hesitated. Kaitlin came around from behind her.

160

"Oh it's you," he said in acknowledgement. "The sisterhood has rallied together, eh?"

Kaitlin stood proud and strong. Shoulders back, staring him directly in the face, very serious. "We don't allow strangers in our homes."

"Well, we're not strangers are we, Kaitlin? Seems we had a chat earlier today. Now let me in, Page," he demanded.

Hesitant, she asked, "W-what is it you want Michael? We can talk through the screen."

"I'm not talking through a goddamn screen like some prisoner. Let me in!" he growled, shaking the screen door on its loose hinges. His face reddened. His eyes pierced.

"I believe you're trespassing, stranger," Quaid said, coming into view a few feet behind the girls, the rifle aimed at the screen door visitor.

There was a momentary flinch of surprise on Michael's face before it turned to anger. Narrowing his eyes and with a snarled lip he growled, "I should've known you'd whore around. You can't make it without a man, can you, Page? This your newest conquest?" He watched her wilt before his eyes. She was milquetoast.

"You've got 10 seconds to state your business, and then I'm going to give you 30 seconds to get off my property," Quaid said evenly, yet threatening.

Michael smirked. "Or what, Mr. Cowboy? You gonna shoot me with that big bad gun?"

"Twenty seconds." The air was tense as each waited for the other to make a move. When Quaid announced ten seconds, Michael backed off.

"I know where you are. I'm not done with you yet, Page." He whirled on his heels and went back to his Lexus slamming the door. He hit the horn with the palm of his hand before gunning the engine. Dust clouds followed him down the long driveway.

"What do we do now, brother?" Kaitlin relaxed her stance as she looked to Quaid for answers.

"I dunno. Let me think on it. Is there anything you haven't told me, Page? Any reason why he thinks he still possesses you?" He put the rifle down to his side and studied her face.

Quaid and Kaitlin looked at the instantaneous change in Page. Like a chastised puppy, her posture slumped, she'd lowered her head, tuned her eyes down, her countenance sober and morose.

"I told you everything. That's Michael. That's what I lived with. One minute he's all suave charm sucking you in, the next, he's Krakatoa—an explosive volcano," she said. "Although, I've never seen him look so poorly," she added quietly. Page sighed deep in defeat. "Can we go home, Kaitlin? I need to pack my things."

"WHAT? You're stronger than this, Page. You're not going to run or hide, are you? You're divorced from the guy; he has no hold over you. Why are you giving in to him?" she scolded.

"You don't understand. . . ." she answered dejectedly. Page looked wistfully out at the plains as if it would be the last time she saw them. "It's what he says. Maybe I am no good. I've never been a strong, assertive woman. I'm weak. I'm humble. I can't even fight back without breaking down in tears." She grabbed a tissue from the box on the table and blew her nose. "I'm not at all like those brave mountain men I read about. I'm just a coward." Tears spilled down her cheeks.

Not knowing whether to be firm or gentle, both sister and brother held their tongues.

Finally, Kaitlin could stand it no longer. "Cowboy up, girl. Didn't you come out here on your own? Didn't you survive CO poisoning? Haven't you struggled to make a life here? You're no coward."

"Words, Page, simply words, he's manipulating you with words. What did you do when you got the thorns in your hand? I pulled them out and you went right out there in the barn—that's grit, that's not cowardice," Quaid added with admiration.

"Yes, but . . . this is different."

"You don't even know what he wants," Quaid argued.

"Me. He wants me. He wants me to be miserable."

"Page Chandling, listen to yourself. You sound like a pathetic waif. Where's your mountain man stamina? Where's your cowgirl guts? We can go home if you want, but you are NOT leaving. Do you understand Page? Don't let him ruin the happiness you've found here."

Page looked up into her friends faces. How could they be so strong? Weren't they scared of Michael? Hadn't they seen his explosive anger? And yet something drastic had happened to him since their divorce. Michael looked awful!

CHAPTER SEVENTEEN

"Open up. I know you're there."

Michael's voice cracked in the still mountain morning. The pounding on Kaitlin Kincaid's door sent tremors through Page. Filled with fear and trepidation the night before, she had returned to Kaitlin's with the purpose of packing out and jumping in her car, driving to somewhere, anywhere. She had bought eight months by coming to Wyoming, maybe she could do it again. Packing quietly in her room until the wee hours of the morning, exhausted, she finally collapsed upon her bed, spending the night dreaming that Michael would snatch her away and she would have to live the hell of an abused woman again. At times the dreams were so vivid she woke in a sweat, her heart beating erratically, silent screams locked in her throat.

And now, the pounding at the door. Should she get up and answer it or let Kaitlin get it? It wasn't her home, even though she'd spent the last six months here.

"Kait? KAIT!" she yelled, hoping her best friend would handle the situation she so wanted to avoid. When silence rebounded, she knew she was on her own. Was Kait not answering on purpose? Donning a bathrobe and running her fingers through her hair, she tried to awaken herself so she would be on her toes for any berating or beguiling charm Michael might impose on her.

"I'm coming," she hollered to the incessant pounding. She opened the door just a crack.

Michael forcefully shoved the door open causing her to step aside as he set foot inside. "Well, well, sunshine so you're not shacked up with that cowboy. Or are you gay now?"

She knew he was watching her for any subtle signs of temerity he could exploit. Seeing him again for the second time within twenty-four hours, she found he wasn't attractive at all anymore. She wondered what she had ever seen in him. Kaitlin's words "Cowboy Up" reverberated in her head. She took a deep breath, squared her shoulders and with all the courage she could muster said, "What is it you want Michael? Our divorce was over months ago."

Michael reached into a breast pocket of his custom tailored suit. Page swallowed hard not knowing what to expect. Did he have a gun? Would he shoot her? She took a step back.

He pulled out an ivory envelope. Holding it up to her she could see it had been addressed to her and had several postal stampings on it where attempts to deliver had failed. She looked at him for some explanation. "What is it?"

"Here, open it," he urged pushing it toward her.

She reached for the envelope, on guard that he could easily grab her wrist and man-handle her. It was the kind of stationery lawyers used. She looked at the return address. It read Michael Chandling, 427 Botsford Lane, Leitchfield, Illinois. Michael had been trying to reach her. For what?

Turning the envelope around in her hands, she slid a finger into the back and opened it. Withdrawing the contents, she read:

Dear Page,

You've probably noticed by the return address I've moved. Shortly after the divorce, I re-married. But Melanie didn't want to live in the house we lived in, so I sold it. By law, you are entitled to half. Enclosed is your half.

Michael

Page stared at the note. She slid the first paper behind the second sheet, which was a signed, notarized copy of a Buy and Sell Agreement. Paper clipped to it was a check for fifty thousand dollars!

Dumbstruck, Page wasn't sure what to say. "I. . . guess congratulations. . . are in order. But, I don't get it. Why hunt me down? "

"May I come in?"

Page had never seen him like this before. His arrogance was gone. His belligerence mellowed. He was a shadow of the man she had known. Was this some kind of calm before the storm? Reluctantly, she allowed him inside. They sat in the living room in silence for a moment or two.

"Are we alone?"

An alarm sounded in her head. What was he up to?

"I-I don't know. I haven't seen Kait."

He looked down at his shoes, then up at Page. "I'm a changed man, Page. I'm sick. . . Dying. . . Cancer. I know now I didn't treat you right and I'm sorry for it. Giving you your half of the house money is probably peanuts for what I put you through."

Page swallowed hard. *Michael dying? Was this another one of his con jobs?* Admittedly, she'd never seen him look so bad. He'd aged terribly. Should she play along or was this her chance to set him straight once and for all? As much as she wanted to tell him off, he looked so small and helpless, so crippled, so ravaged. She felt a twinge of pity. Looking at him, it was unbelievable he could change so much. She silently prayed she wasn't making a mistake as she said, "Cancer? Dying? How? When?"

"I guess I had it even when we were still together. It wasn't until I went for a blood test to marry Melanie they found out something was wrong. It's pancreatic and it's fatal. So, you won't have to worry about me hurting you anymore."

Tears sprang to her eyes. Michael was dying! "I-I'm so sorry, "she whispered in muffled tones. She wanted to ask how long he had, but couldn't bring herself to do so. She looked down the papers in her hands. "Shouldn't Melanie have this money?"

"Melanie comes from money. She has more than she needs. No, this, this is for you Page, with my love."

"Y-Your love?" The tears crested her cheeks. This was all so unreal.

"I do love you, Page. I always have. I guess I just never knew how to show it. I was afraid it would make me look weak. Now, well, now it doesn't matter, does it? I'm dying. I suppose you're wondering why I came all the way out here. You can see I tried mailing it. After it came back two or three times, and after I got my death sentence, I had to see you face-to-face, one last time. I had to be sure you got the money. I hired a private investigator to find you. The rest is history. Here I am and there's your money."

Defeat shrouded him. She could see it with her eyes. Hear it with her ears. Pent up pain from years of abuse plus the news of his impending death swelled within her. Tears streaked her face. Was she crying for him or for herself?

"Hey, none of that. I don't want your pity. I just had to make things right for once and for all."

She looked over at the shell of a man she'd once been married to. Head and heart tumbled emotions— sorrow, relief, pity, compassion. It was one of those awkward moments when one didn't know what to say.

"I'll be on my way now. I was wondering—could you—would you—be willing to kiss me one last time?" He stood and awaited her answer.

A rush of sadness and compassion filled her. What harm could it do? She went over to him and wrapped her arms around him, all the while on guard he could wrap his arms around her and she would be held captive.

Flinching and drawing back, he said, "Don't, don't hug me. It hurts too much. Just a kiss."

She realized this might be the last time she ever kissed his lips, ever seen him alive. Drawing herself to him, without touching, she neared his mouth, smelling the decay and drugs. His hands came up to her face and for a moment she was frightened he might crush her between them, but just as quickly realized all his strength and bravado was gone. He kissed her gently, without passion, before turning to walk out of her life.

CHAPTER EIGHTEEN

Page wasn't sure what to feel; a lingering melancholy stayed with her for several days after Michael's leaving. On the other hand, she felt a tremendous lightening, physically and mentally. She was free! No more being afraid. No more jumping at shadows. No more walking on pins and needles. Free to live her life as she pleased. Free to love again. But, how would she know it wasn't a trick?

Finally, she called the realtor on the Buy and Sell Agreement who verified the sale of the property. Next, she called the bank the check was drawn on and they verified the funds. No falsehoods, no tricks, no bogus check. Stunned to have fifty-thousand dollars thrown in her lap, she set the check on her bedside table where she could see it each morning and every night before going to bed. Fifty-thousand! Somewhere, somehow, there was a kernel of goodness in Michael after all. But what should she do with all that money?

*   *   *   *

Warm smells of horseflesh, hay, leather and oil met Page as she went through the large barn doors. Looking around she heard Quaid talking in one of the horse stalls. She wondered whom he could be talking to. Windrunner whinnied seeing Page.

"Hey!" Quaid said as the gelding shied away. Alert to the horse's behavior, Quaid swerved around catching a glimpse of Page. "What brings you out here?"

"I just wanted to see you," she said.

"I thought you'd be headed for Leitchfield," he grunted as he held the gelding's hoof in one hand while with the other he used a hoof pick to dig and scrape around the foot.

He was back to the cold, austere Quaid of months ago. Page, now well aware of his jealous streak aimed to pacify him, "I'm not going to Leitchfield. Not now. Not ever."

"Not ever?" He looked up at her. "What'd Michael want?"

"Kaitlin didn't tell you?"

"Tell me what?"

Very quietly she spoke. "Michael's dying. Cancer."

"And he came out here . . . for what?"

"He needed to see me." She paused not sure whether to tell him about the money. Deciding it was unnecessary, she commented no further.

He dropped the horse's foot, stood erect, and looked at her. "I'm sorry," he murmured." Are you all right?"

She nodded. "Can I help?"

"Cleaning hooves is a dirty, stinking job. Are you sure you're up to it?"

"You bet. Will you show me how?"

Quaid shook his head. "Just remember, you asked."

She let him manipulate her into position behind the horse's left foreleg, listening intently as he instructed her.

Page wrinkled her nose at the fetid smell arising. "You're right, it stinks."

Quaid came in for a closer look. "Looks like thrush. We'll have to wash her out, pack it with iodine soaked cotton balls."

"Will she be all right?" she asked, concerned for the animal's welfare.

"Probably. I just don't have time to do everything that needs tending to around here. She's probably been out in the wet mud too long. Kind of hard this time of year with the snow run off. Pastures can be wet. Corral is a mess."

"Ohhhhhhhh, I feel like I'm hurting her," Page said, wincing.

"Naw, they're pretty tough, 'cept for the frog there. Would you rather I did it? You can find some iodine and cotton balls in the tack room. Soak 'em good. I'll pack her."

Page went to find the first aid supplies.

*   *   *   *

The 25th of May another fluke blizzard hit. The wind whipped the tall cottonwoods near the creek until it looked as if they would snap in two. Screeching like an insane woman, snow whirled and danced through the air obscuring everything in sight. Relieved to finish plowing the road with plenty of time to spare, Quaid saddled up and rode out into the northeast pasture to check the livestock.

He squint his eyes against the spitting snow, trying to count the stock. A plaintive bawling rose through the air. There she stood near a lone aspen calling out to her calf. He frantically searched the plain for its mother before moseying Windrunner through the powdery snow to the edge of the plain where it dropped off into a basin.

"Damn! Don't you die on me, " swore Quaid, as he located the young bull standing shivering in the ice-cold half-frozen creek.

Windrunner minced his steps down the incline only losing his footing once, only to quickly regain it.

Roping the young cow around the neck, he wrapped the other end around the saddle horn and instructed Windrunner to pull. Bawling, the little guy balked. "Git, c'mon, git cow, " he yelled. He jumped into the icy water and pushed its rear end while Windrunner backed up, pulling. Normally, the calf would get the message and with leaps and bounds free itself, but not this one. The young bull's watering eyes just looked at him before folding its legs, falling over, wet and frozen. Quaid took his hat off, beating his leg with it, cursing.

Mindful this was only one and the rest of the herd was out, he had no choice but to leave the calf and go round up the remainder. He herded as many as he could trailing homeward behind them.

By the time he neared the ranch house Kait was in the yard, the truck still running. Seeing him, she jumped out of the truck and ran to the gate. As Quaid brought up the rear and the last cow was inside, she swung the gate shut.

"That all of them?" she asked, peering over the fence rail, trying to get a count.

A worried look creased his face. "Calf out. The heifer. I'm going back out." He turned Windrunner around and headed back out. If he lost the new heifer, he wasn't sure what he would do.

"Do you want me to follow?" she yelled.

"Stay here."

* * * *

172

Page's Taurus slipped and slid on the winding road to the ranch house. She was thankful Quaid had put chains on the tires; in addition, her driving skills were improving. Stopping near the house, she noticed Kaitlin out by the corral. She jumped out of her car and ran over to her.

"Hi. What's going on?" Steam rose from her breath in the air.

"Cow's in trouble. Quaid just brought these in. But the heifer calf is missing."

Being a city girl, Page didn't understand the dangers of the cattle being out, but saw worry written all over Kaitlin's face. "Aren't cows tough? What could happen to them? "

"If you only knew. Poor things. They can be so dumb. They'll get lost in this blizzard. If they get into the creek they can freeze. If it ices over they can cut their hooves, cut their noses."

"I know Quaid told me to stay here, but I've got to help him. That little girl's in trouble."

"I want to go too. Six eyes are better than two," Page said eagerly.

The truck rolled through the snow in the opposite direction from where Quaid had ridden off.

"I can't see a thing past the hood. What if we run into it? " Page sat on the edge of the seat, chewing her lip, straining to see through the heavy snow and steamy windshield.

"We better not is all I can say."

The wind swirled the large flakes in tornado-like fury. The wipers clogged with heavy wet snow before they cleared the glass. Kaitlin stopped several times manually brushing the snow off while they crept through the pasture. The headlights, snow covered, shone at half their brilliancy.

"Kait? There's a big shape over that way. " Page pointed.

Kait turned the truck and proceeded cautiously. "Yep! That's her. Oh God, no."

"What? What is it?" Page asked anxiously. When the truck stopped, she moved her head back and forth trying to make out the scene before her.

Kaitlin jumped out of the truck. She ran over to the calf lying in the snow. Kait stood there for a few minutes, head bowed.

Page noticed the pain and distress etched on Kaitlin's face when she returned to the truck.

"It's frozen."

"Noooooooo." Page's tender heart ached.

With a deep breath, Kaitlin grabbed a rope, went back to the calf, lassoed it around the neck, and tied the other end to the tow ball at the back of the truck. Jumping back in the truck, she stared straight ahead. "Let's go home. There's enough snow, she'll skim over the top of it. We'll drop her off in the bone yard," Kait said.

The short drive back seemed twice as long with heavy hearts and silent speech.

Two hours later, Quaid dragged his weary body into the house. Page and Kait sat drinking coffee at the kitchen table. He noticed the morose look on Kaitlin's face and Page's swollen eyes revealed she'd been crying. He dusted himself off before pouring himself a cup of the warm brew and collapsing in one of the chairs.

"I'm so sorry, Quaid," Kaitlin murmured. "We found her frozen." She choked on the words. "She's in the bone yard."

"I know," he said quietly, "I saw her there when I took the little bull."

"No, not the bull too. Oh, Quaid." She fell silent knowing no words would help Quaid over the loss.

"I'm-I'm sorry too, Quaid," Page said through her crying.

"God damn it!" He beat his fists on the table. The cash he'd get from them was gone. Defeated, he wondered if he shouldn't give up ranching altogether. What was the use? For every step he took forward two steps pulled him back. He rose from the table. He went to the bedroom and quietly shut the door, relieved the girls were nowhere near to see how badly he was hurting.

CHAPTER NINETEEN

Quaid came out some time later. Going over to the roll-top desk, he didn't say a word to either of them. He riffled through the stack of unpaid bills on the desk, scratched at the stubble growing on his face, shook his head, and with quiet defeat said, "I'm done, Kait. I've tried and tried to make a go of it. Denise tore me down financially. I can't keep ahead of the game. I can't get ahead for trying. Seems like I'm selling off more than what I got. Losing those new heifers means there's no breeding stock. . ."

"I could sell the Aladdin house, come back here to live. That would bring in some income." Kaitlin walked over to her brother and laid a sympathetic hand on his shoulder.

"I can't ask you to do that. Besides, you hate ranching. You put up with it when Mom and Pop were around 'cause you were little and had to do chores. And don't think I don't appreciate all the help you've given me since. But, it's not enough, Kait, it's just not enough."

She pulled up a chair and sat across from him. "I love you, Quaid. You're my brother. I'd do anything for you. I haven't minded helping out too much. Although if I had my druthers- ," she chuckled. "But, I wanted to see you make a go of things. I've watched you struggle as everything has turned against you. You don't deserve that. You've worked so hard. This is your big dream, Quaid. And because we're all that's left of family there's no reason for me to live in Aladdin when I could just as well live here. It wouldn't be like losing my inheritance if I sold out and invested it in the ranch."

"I can't ask you to do that, sis. It's time you got on with your own life. Find yourself a husband, have a family. You shouldn't be stuck helping me fulfill my dreams." Quaid hung his head in his hands, silent.

Page, quietly observing up to that moment, cheerfully offered, "Let's brainstorm ways to make money."

In a snap she saw Kaitlin frown before taking her aside.

"Not now, Page," she say in a hushed tone so her brother couldn't hear. "You see, each calf is important. One bull can breed many heifers, but the heifers increase the herd. This is turn increases sales which means more cash for purchasing more head, feed, ranch maintenance and paying bills. Losing the calves is losing a cash crop."

"But I just—" Before she could finish her sentence, Kaitlin interrupted.

"Would you go feed Blue and Chester, please? We forgot all about them. "

When she was gone, Kaitlin walked over to her brother. Looking over his shoulder she said, "She's just trying to take your mind off things. She thinks she's helping."

"I made my bed, now I'll have to lie in it," he said restlessly pacing the floor, looking out the window. "It's going to kill me to give this up. What would Mom and Pop think, me losing the ranch an' all?" Taking a deep breath, he let it out. "I'll have to call Marty at High Plains Realty tomorrow."

"Quaid, please, don't be so impulsive. Surely, something can be done. Besides, what would you do? Where would you go?"

At that instant, Page returned. "I overheard . . . you can't give up the ranch. You just can't."

Silence filled the room.

* * * *

Page stared at the fifty-thousand dollar check on her nightstand. For the past few days, she had mulled over different ways of investing it, spending it, saving it. All at once, she knew what she wanted to do with it. That afternoon she walked into the quietly shoved the check towards the teller.

"I want to apply forty-thousand of that on Quaid Kincaid's loan."

Marg, the teller looked at the check, her eyes growing big, then to Page. "We can't cash this, ma'am. We'd have to wait seven to ten days for the check to clear." She looked at the check then back to Page. "Did you say you wanted to apply it to a loan?"

"Yes, Quaid Kincaid's. I don't see why—"

"Is there a problem here?"

The next thing Page knew, a burly, ruddy faced man walked up to her. The teller handed him the check.

"Ms. Chandling? I'm Martin Farnsworth. Senior Vice President." He extended a large meaty hand. Shaking her hand, he slipped his other hand behind her back and directed her away from the tellers' booths over to his desk. "It's not everyday we get a request like this." He motioned for her to take a seat. After she sat down he continued, "That's a lot of money for a stranger to be putting on a loan. Particularly when it's not *your* loan."

"Yes, sir, but the bank doesn't care who pays the money, as long as the loan is fulfilled, do they?"

"Well— ahem— technically no, but. . . We know Quaid around here quite well and being aware of his financial status, we, uh . . . Just what is your relationship to Mr. Kincaid? Does Quaid know you're doing this?"

"Not just yet, but he will."

"Your relationship?"

"Fiancée," she blurted. *Whew boy! Where did that come from?*

"It's like this, Ms. Chandling, I can't stop you from doing it, but you realize we'll have to wait ten days for the check to clear."

"The check is good, Mr. Farnsworth, I've already checked with the bank."

"Nevertheless—"

Page shook his hand and heaved a heavy, exasperated sigh. "You'd think in today's world of telephones and computers this kind of thing would be almost instantaneous." She arose, shook Mr. Farnsworth's extended hand again and proceeded to the teller's window to deposit the money.

Step one, successful. With ten thousand left she should be able to buy some cattle. She reported for work and before Mr. Siler, her boss, arrived in the office, she made a phone call to Jake Stoner. Relieved to find Jake held no hostility toward her for breaking up, after preliminaries, she presented him with a request: "I know this is asking a lot, but I was wondering if you could help me. I need to purchase a couple of calves."

He chuckled. "What have you gotten yourself into?"

"I can't disclose my plans. And you have to swear to secrecy. It has to be a surprise for Quaid. But I sure would be grateful if you'd help me out here."

"You realize he's not going to take to this."

"What do you mean?"

"He's proud. He's going to know something is fishy."

"I'll deal with that later. How soon can we get them?"

"Should be an auction tonight at the stockyard. Seven p.m."

"I'll be ready and waiting," she said eagerly.

"Out of friendship, I'll do it. But you realize he's going to raise holy hell when we come haulin' cattle up his drive."

* * * *

The next day, Quaid watched the cattle hauler come barreling up the drive. Must be the cattle buyer I called yesterday. Quaid walked out of the house as the vehicle pulled up nearby. Seeing Jake Stoner he tensed. Then he saw the Taurus.

Jake stopped short of a corral, opened the door of his truck and hollered out, "Where do you want these babies?"

Next, Page jumped out of her car.

"What the hell is going on?" he muttered. He approached the big cowman walking towards him. "Jake." He nodded in greeting, tipping his hat slightly.

"Quaid." Jake did likewise.

"Let's get these calves unloaded," Page said.

"Hold on there! What calves?" Quaid asked.

"Your new calves," Jake said, watching Quaid's expression.

Surly, he answered, "I didn't buy any calves."

"No, but I did," Page said. "Should we turn 'em loose in the pasture or the corral?"

Quaid stood, hands on hips, looking at her as if she'd been smoking jimson weed. "What in tarnation do you think you're doing?"

"I bought a couple of heifers. Thought you'd let me board 'em here. I'll pay for food, vet, whatever. Maybe your bull could breed them when they're ready."

"Are you crazy? Where'd they come from?" *Damn her, how dare she do something like this without asking first? And what was Jake doing in the equation?*

"Got the papers right here." Jake reached in his breast pocket to give them to Page when Quaid intercepted them.

Quaid glanced through the papers. Everything was in order. What was he going to do with new calves when he'd listed the remaining stock at the auction barn and the ranch with High Plains earlier today? He had to get rid of his stock not add to it. He'd been on the phone all morning with neighboring ranchers about buying him out. With more than a hint of impatience and irritation he took a hold of her arm and led her aside.

"Just what do you think you are doing?" Quaid demanded.

Smugly, she answered, "I'm going to raise cattle."

"What for?"

"You've converted me. I want to be a cattle rancher," she said boldly. "Well, are you just going to stand there or are you going to help me?"

In a difficult situation, Quaid motioned for Jake to unload them through the chute at the corral. *What the hell is going on?* He watched Page as she went to help unload the calves. We've got to have a serious talk.

"You couldn't've picked a worse time to buy cattle. I'm sellin' the ranch. Sellin' the cattle," he said minutes later after Jake had left and she walked into the house.

Crestfallen, Page stopped midstream. "Y-you have a buyer already?"

"Spoke to a guy on the phone. I thought that was him comin' up the drive."

"You're going to show the ranch yourself?"

"What? I'm talkin' about a buyer for the rest of the beeves."

"Y-You're selling off your cattle?"

"No choice," he said.

Page heard the tired in his voice, saw the defeat on his face. "But, I. . ."

"You're going to have to sell those calves off or find someplace else to keep 'em. Furthermore, what the hell are you doin' with Jake Stoner again? I thought we had something goin'." His face reddened. His jaw tensed.

Page saw the ire rising. She couldn't afford to lose him now that everything was turning around in her life. Should she tell him what she was up to? "Oh, all right," she said with a trace of irritation in her voice. "You know, you're just a spoiled sport. It was supposed to be a surprise. I know how bad you felt losing your calves, so I wanted to replace them."

"Now why would you do a thing like that?"

"Why? Do I have to spell it out for you? I care about you. I love you. When you hurt, I hurt. Do you think I want you to lose this ranch? I love it here. I've always wanted a ranch, but I can never afford one. That's why I'm going to make you a proposition. Marry me Quaid, and we'll make this ranch work together."

He simply stared at her totally bamboozled.

CHAPTER TWENTY

Marry her? Had he heard right? Shy, quiet, little Page proposing to him? Where had all this newfound confidence come from? He couldn't marry her. He wasn't marriage material. He was broke. He'd already listed the ranch with the realtor. Calls were in for selling his stock. Marry her? That was pretty bold on her part. If he hadn't been so jolted, he'd have told her so. Confused and feeling a twinge of jealousy, he decided before he did anything impulsive, he needed to get away and think. He walked past her, past the new heifers in the corral, out to the barn where he saddled Windrunner.

* * * *

All the way to Rapid, she talked to herself aloud, surprised she had so boldly asserted herself. Would it scare Quaid away? Would he take her proposal seriously? Did she know Quaid and her own heart well enough to plunge into something so drastic? She realized she'd been attracted to him since she'd seen him in the hospital. Taken aback by his surliness she now understood what lie behind it— frustration and disappointment. Besides, maybe he was changing. But, changing or not, she loved him and she would do anything for him.

Once at work, Page found it difficult to concentrate on her duties. In spare moments, she found herself doodling the name Mrs. Quaid Kincaid and every other variation she could think of on scratch pads like a love struck adolescent. How long would it take Quaid to make up his mind? Excited, antsy and edgy all at the same time, at lunchtime she decided to go for a walk. Maybe it would calm her down.

DOUBLE K RANCH FOR SALE. 550 ACRES NESTLED IN FOOTHILLS OF BLACK HILLS. FENCED PASTURE,SMALL HOME AND BARN, CORRAL.MUST SELL. OWNER WILLING TO LOOK AT ALL OFFERS. CONTACT MARTY MONTGOMERY, HIGH PLAINS REAL ESTATE, 857-4214 OR QUAID KINCAID 857-5151.

The flyer in the window caught her eye. No! This couldn't be. He was advertising the ranch! How could he do that when she was working so feverishly to save it? She looked at the sign on the door: HIGH PLAINS REALTY WHERE WE MAKE YOUR DREAMS COME TRUE. A mix of anger and distress swelled within her.

She stormed inside only to find the office empty. She went over to the window and ripped off the ad, startled when a woman's voice came from behind her. She jumped.

"Can I help you?" A tall, slim woman appeared in a paisley bandana print blouse tucked neatly within a blue denim skirt; her navy blue cowboy boots looked new. She wore a contrasting red bandana around her neck. Her lanky brown hair hung straight to her shoulders. It was difficult to judge her age for the sun had worn deep furrows and crow's feet in her face.

"*What* is this?" Page said, waving the ad in front of the realtor's face.

Affronted, the realtor stepped back and swung her arm out in the direction of her workstation before saying anything. She motioned for Page to sit across from her. "Would you care for a soda or coffee?"

"No thank you. Just tell me about this ad," she demanded.

The realtor, whose nameplate read Marty Montgomery, scanned the ad quickly. "Oh, this is a lovely property over near. . ."

"I know where it is. Is this the official listing?" Page demanded.

Marty shook her head. "No. We talked with Mr. Kincaid and his sister about listing, but they wanted to try selling it themselves first. I just agreed to let him put the ad in our window. Mr. Kincaid is a very proud man; I could see how much it was hurting him to give up the ranch. Of course, no one, well hardly anyone, takes these owner postings serious. It was just a way of letting him come to terms with things."

Page perked up while relaxing her defensiveness. "It's not a legal listing then?"

"Actually, yes and no. It's not Hoyle for our office, but if Mr. Kincaid can find a buyer and do the paperwork, then yes, it would be binding."

"Did he say how long he was going to advertise it himself?"

"Why no, but usually a couple of weeks is about right. After that, the truth sets in and he probably will come to us." She studied Page. "Are you interested in the property?"

"Very. Is there any way to delay listing it?"

Marty looked at Page curiously. "Are you family? Is there some dispute?"

"Yes. I'm a sister." She lied straight-faced. *Oh God, where did that come from?*

"That's odd," the woman said frowning. "We know just about everyone in these parts and neither Quaid nor Kaitlin have ever mentioned another sister. But, you're not from around here, are you?"

"That's right. I'm from Minnesota. I was adopted out as a baby. It's just recently that I found my family records. When I found that Quaid and Kait were living here, I came out to find them and be reunited." *Geez, I'm just a babbling fountain of lies. Is she going to fall for this?* "I'm sure neither of the Kincaids is even aware of my presence yet."

"Let me call Mr. Kincaid and tell him you're here in the office," Ms. Montgomery said picking up her phone.

Shaking her head vehemently, Page said, "No, no. Don't do that. I . . . I want to surprise them and besides meeting here . . ." She looked around the office. ". . . somehow doesn't seem right. Please, don't call. I'll go to the ranch and talk with them." She rose and started for the door. As an afterthought, she added, "Please don't sell this out from under me. It should stay in the family."

"Wait. I'll give you the address and draw you a map." The woman began flipping through her Rolodex.

"That's all right. I'll find it," Page called over her shoulder glimpsing the look of dismay on Marty's face before hurrying out the door.

*   *   *   *

"Morning, Mr. Farnsworth." Quaid tipped his hat to the bank manager who stood and nodded for Quaid to take a seat. Shifting his lanky frame into the leather chair, Quaid began: "It seems like a serious mistake has been made. I came in to get the payoff on my loan. Gonna have to sell the place. But something's wrong here. These figures don't jive with my records." He shoved a ledger over on the desk so Farnsworth could see.

Farnsworth reached out and drew the ledger to him, skimmed the figures. What should he say? He recalled the perky little blond that had been in a few days earlier to pay on the account. It was hard to forget a customer with $40,000. Surely, she had told Quaid by this time.

"Drastic difference in our figures, Farnsworth. I don't like blaming anyone unfairly, but one of your tellers has made a big mistake."

Farnsworth hated to be the one to let the cat out of the bag, especially if the large deposit was to be a surprise. Yet, ethically he couldn't keep the disclosure secret.

"No sir, Quaid, it's no mistake. There was a $40,000 deposit made upon your loan. I, uh, ahem, thought your fiancée would have told you."

Quaid came to full alert. "Fiancée? What are you talking about, Farnsworth?"

"Seems as though your fiancée came in about a week or so ago and insisted on paying on your loan. I thought it a little strange, but, bottom line, the bank is only interested the loan is paid. Doesn't rightly matter who pays on it." He looked at the surprise on Quaid's face. "I, uh, thought she would have told you about it by now. Guess it was supposed to be a surprise."

Quaid sat floored by the news. *Who? Page. What is she up to?*

"Congratulations, Quaid. Seems like a nice woman. About time you re-married." Farnsworth's meaty hand reached out to shake Quaid's.

Quaid nodded his head and rose, dazed.

CHAPTER TWENTY-ONE

Quaid sat in his truck trying to make sense of what was happening. New calves, a substantial payment on his loan, a marriage proposal? What did Page think she was doing? It was time this came to a halt. He turned the key in the ignition and set out for Rapid City.

He stormed into Siler, Jones and Krauthammer.

"May I help you?" A tall brunette woman in the reception area asked.

"Where's Page?"

"Page? I assume you mean Page Chandling? She was called out of the office unexpectedly. Is there something I can help you with?"

"Called out where?"

"I really don't know and if I did I wouldn't be at liberty to tell you."

Fuming, Quaid turned on his heels and stormed back out the door. "Where in hell is she? If she's with Jake Stoner, I'll . . ." he muttered.

* * * *

"Thank you. Thank you. Thank you so much for coming." Melanie Chandling, dressed in black, with a small veil, stood near the casket receiving visitors. Sprays of flowers in various arrangements filled the room. Upon seeing Page, she walked up to her. "Thank you so much for coming, Page. It really wasn't necessary, but if Michael . . ." Melanie broke into tears. Regaining some composure, she continued, "It means a lot."

Page couldn't figure out how it could mean much to Melanie, a woman she had never met before. And it certainly didn't mean anything to Michael. It was just one of those things people said in these circumstances. She nodded before walking up to the casket. She paused a moment before taking a seat for the services. As she sat waiting for the service to begin, the years she'd spent with Michael flowed through her mind. And now it was truly over. When she had gotten the call that he had passed away, she'd wrestled with her feelings for days. Finally, convicted to show her last respects to a man who had shown her little respect, she booked the first flight she could get back to Leitchfield, Illinois.

The minister's words were drowned out by her own thoughts. As if a jailer had unlocked a prison cell door, she felt unshackled, light. Unburdened, she was no longer under the weight of Michael's dominance. She was finally free to have the life she wanted. Almost. Her thoughts turned to Quaid. Had he sold the ranch yet? It would take time for the paperwork to go through, wouldn't it? Had he thought about her proposal?

"Please come to the house and eat with us," Melanie asked when the service had ended. "We should only be a few minutes at the cemetery."

"No, thank you. I have to get back to Wyoming. I hope everything will be all right for you." Page gave her a light hug before taking leave.

189

Page couldn't have eaten a thing even if she were hungry. With so much happening so fast, Page's nerves were frazzled. Her stomach upset at various times of the day, she questioned if she had a mild case of food poisoning. Then again, it might be her sporadic eating habits of late. At times, she felt lightheaded, other times slightly nauseated. Certain she would calm down and feel better once she heard whether Quaid would marry her or not, she pulled into a convenience store and bought a box of saltine crackers and a ginger ale. Chewing on saltines seemed to be the only thing that set well in her stomach.

*　*　*　*

Where was she? He'd called Jake only to be surprised not to find her there. Then he'd called Kaitlin. She didn't know what was going on either. Just that Page had left town unexpectedly. Did she intend to come back?

With nothing to do but chores and waiting for the realtor to call with an offer, he had lots of time to think. Here was a woman who'd come into his life in a snowstorm. An unlikely candidate for a rancher's wife, she'd wormed her way into his life and heart without him being fully aware of it. He recalled her willingness to help at the ranch without complaint. She'd endured the pain of physical labor, the mental agony of losing stock, the harshness of eking out a living in Wyoming. Her fears of her ex-husband had exacerbated themselves unnecessarily. He was dying. He would be out of her life for good. With that fear gone, maybe she would be more relaxed. It suddenly dawned on him they'd had intercourse twice without the benefit of contraception. He should have known better. But then, she was probably on the pill or had an intrauterine device. She had given herself spontaneously and unselfishly. Just as she had unselfishly bought calves and made payment on his dreams. Wasn't that the kind of

190

woman he'd been waiting for? Wasn't it time to admit he loved her? Could the two of them make a go of ranching?

"That's right. I want to back out of the sale," Quaid said to Marty Montgomery a short time later. "I won't be listing with you after all."

As he hung up the phone, he hoped to hell he didn't regret it.

CHAPTER TWENTY-TWO

He'd paced the floors and worried around the clock until Kaitlin called that Page had arrived home. He immediately asked to speak with her.

"Page, I'd like for you to come out to the ranch tonight. We need to talk."

Pleased she'd said yes, he had a lot of making up to do. He went out and saddled Windrunner, then rode out to the pastures. After making sure all was well with the cattle, he set out to where he had first picked prairie roses for her. He picked a large bunch and came back to the ranch where he found an old mayonnaise jar, filled it with water and set the roses in it. He cleared off the kitchen table and placed the roses in the center of it.

He pulled antelope steaks out of the freezer and found a couple of large baking potatoes. Scouring the cupboards, he found a can of corn and another of applesauce. He set them on the counter and went to shower.

Clean in a fresh, sky blue shirt with pearl snaps and dress jeans, he threw an apron over him and set to cooking. He looked at the clock. She'd be arriving anytime. He looked at the table. Something was missing. Quickly, he began scrambling through the roll-top desk, kitchen drawers, looking everywhere. Finding a lone candle, he stuck it in the middle of the roses. It canted to the right and rolled on the lip of the jar. He ran out the back door and began searching through the dirt. Finding a half dozen stones, he brought them in and removing the roses, plunked the rocks in the bottom of the jar, replaced the candle which now stood upright and set the roses back in water.

Apprehensive, Page steered the Taurus up the familiar drive to the ranch house. Had Quaid made his decision? Perhaps she had been out of line buying the calves and making the loan payment. Maybe there was some unwritten Wyoming rule about that too. But it was too late to undo. And if Quaid was going to rail against her, so be it. She would have to accept that and get on with her life without him.

Taking a deep breath, setting her resolve, she walked in to the ranch house.

"Quaid? I'm here," she called out.

"In the kitchen," he hollered back. Afterward he walked out with his hands held out like a surgeon awaiting gloves, his hands coated with flour paste. He came over to her and pecked her on the cheek. "Dinner will be ready in a few minutes."

Page couldn't help but smile; seeing Quaid in an apron seemed out of character. Dinner? She followed him into the kitchen. Surprise shone on her face seeing the table set, the candle glowing, the bouquet of roses.

"I'd seat you, but my hands are full right now," he said wiggling them in the air.

"That's all right. What are you making? Need help?" She went over to where he stood at the stove.

"No, ma'am." He went to the sink, washed his hands. Next, he guided her to a seat. Within minutes, he placed dinner in front of her. "Hope you like it." He sat down across from her.

"Umm, what is this? It doesn't taste quite like beef. But it is so tender. It's just wonderful."

"Antelope steak a la Kincaid."

"Oh my, another first for me."

"Seems like you've had a lot of firsts since coming to Wyoming."

"Yes, I guess I have." When was he going to rail against her for up and leaving? Or was he going to give her his answer? She was quiet for a few moments before venturing, "I guess, I'll need to take those calves back to auction. I don't suppose you'd help me do that, would you, Quaid?"

"I could, but I won't."

Let down, she told herself she was only getting what she deserved. "Don't worry about the money on the loan. I just. . . made a bad investment."

"Only bad if you think so," he said in between bites.

She wasn't sure she was following the conversation. Attempting a different approach she ventured, "Have you sold the ranch yet?"

"Nope, and I sure as hell don't want to." He rose and came back with dishes of applesauce. "I know one thing. I sure can't make a go of it alone." He fell silent working on the dessert. Afterwards, he set the spoon down quietly as he looked at her; he reached his hand across the table over to hers where she was setting her spoon aside.

"I want you. I want you so bad, Page Chandling."

"I want you too, Quaid." Was that his answer?

All thoughts of losing the ranch drifted away as they made passionate love under starlit Wyoming skies. Page lay in Quaid's arms fulfilled and happy for the first time in years. A wonderful lover, he had been as tender this time as the previous times. Tender with just the right amount of roughness. As she lay luxuriating in the subtle smells of aftershave, perfume and sex scented sheets, she realized they had not used any protection again. They were getting much too careless. Never being able to get pregnant by Michael, she assumed there was something wrong with her ability to conceive and therefore didn't give contraception much thought. Now, the question loomed in her mind as she scrunched under the covers for another minute of afterglow.

* * * *

"Do you feel well enough to go for a ride this morning?" Quaid asked.

Page came out of the bathroom, her face ashen. "Yeah, sure, I guess I just picked up a bug."

"Breakfast?" he said, rising from the bed where Page had lain down again.

"Ugh, no. I don't suppose you have any crackers?"

"Sorry. Why don't you rest while I go saddle up the horses?"

"Okay."

When was he going to give her a decision? Should she give him an ultimatum? All this anticipation was causing butterflies in her stomach. After Quaid left, she went to her purse and took out a pregnancy kit. It seemed rather foolish, yet she had had this bug for too long. She followed the instructions and then dressed to go riding. Before leaving the house, she checked the test.

Oh my God, I'm pregnant. Beaming with the thought of having Quaid's baby, it was only when Quaid returned to tell her the horses were saddled and ready that her thoughts went sour. *What if he doesn't marry me? What if he doesn't want this baby?* The joy of going riding was suddenly fraught with worry.

Cresting a butte, they stopped, dismounting to look out over the expanse of land. The wide panorama always put her in awe. "Umm, I could live here forever," she said breathing in the high altitude air, scanning the blue cloudless horizon.

He smiled. "Do you realize how many times you've told me that? What is it with you? I never thought a city girl would be crazy about Wyoming."

She faced him. "It's a feeling of freedom. Even though it makes me feel very small in the grand scheme of things, it soothes me; it makes me feel free to be me. It lifts my spirits and makes me want to take it all in. And . . . promise you will not laugh? I just feel good about life out here. I feel spiritual, at one with creation and God."

She watched as he leaned over to kiss her. Their lips meeting, she felt his tongue glide between her teeth, exploring the regions of her mouth, going deeper and deeper. An infusion of heat rose within her. Resistance melted as rising passion filled her. Warmth tingled from her head to her toes. She returned his kisses in wild abandonment, grasping at his back and shoulders, pulling him closer and closer. At that moment, all she wanted was Quaid's love.

As his hands slid around her buttocks, pulling her up tight against him, she saw the love lust in his eyes, felt the hunger in his kisses, as his hard erection pressed against her belly.

Breaking away, he pulled a bedroll blanket off his horse and threw it down on the ground. Reaching for her hands, he pulled her down to the blanketed earth.

"Quaid, we can't do it here."

Husky voiced, full of lust, he said, "Do you see anybody around here? It's just the two of us with the birds and the bees."

She felt him unbutton her blouse, slide his hand up under her bra, pushing it upward he circled the areole

196

before laving her nipples. Carried away by the pleasurable feeling, she was barely aware of his hand unzipping her jeans, reaching his hand down to her most private area, feeling her wetness. On fire, she helped him inch her jeans off. His hands removed her panties. Lying naked, he kissed every inch of her, and then returned to her warm opening. He massaged her mons until she was moaning. When she felt she could take no more, she whispered, "Take me." He entered her, and slowly rocked back and forth until she gasped in orgasm and fireworks exploded before her eyes. She felt him come in her and realized she no longer had to worry about pregnancy. But she wondered if this was a good time to tell Quaid about the baby.

They dressed quickly, but lay on the blanket basking in the afterglow, finding cloud figures. He gazed at her as the sun shone on her blonde hair gently blowing in the breeze. Her face glowed. Tiny crow's feet were beginning to etch around her eyes. Her once pale skin had tanned. It didn't matter to him if she had crow's feet or leathery skin; he loved her and would love her all the days of his life.

He said, "I did a lot of thinkin' while you were gone. I've decided to go into partnership on the ranch." He paused looking over at her for her reaction.

"Partnership?" *Had he found a buyer that wanted to go into partnership with him?*

"You sold the ranch?" she asked.

Stoic he lay looking up at the blue Wyoming sky. "It's not final yet. But my partner's already helped a heap, what with buyin' calves, makin' partial payment. . ."

Was he talking about her? On the other hand, had something transpired while she was away?

Her smile crumpled as she attempted to masquerade her disappointment. "That's great."

He turned to face her. Then rose, placing his Stetson on his head. Bending down on one knee, he removed the hat again so she could see his face as he solemnly asked, "Would you be my partner?"

"A partner? That's not exactly what I had in mind. I'm afraid I'm not following you." She sat up erect.

He swiped his face with his hand. "Geez, you gonna make me say the exact words?" He hung his head uncomfortable with the proposition, although it was what his heart had wanted for some time.

"I love you, Page Chandling. Reckon I have ever since I brought you out to the ranch and you fell in love with it. I've been a real ass about everything. Couldn't imagine a woman wanting this," he spread his arms out and looked across the land. "But come to think on it, you've turned into a ranch woman and you're not that shy little thing I picked out of a snowstorm no more. Anyone that would go to all the trouble you did must have a care for me." The words came hard for him, but he had to make her see that he wanted her and loved her as much as she loved him. "I reckon you had to do what you had to do to get around this ol' stubborn mule. Page Chandling, would you marry this broken down cowboy even though I haven't got a thing to offer you?"

Partner? Marry? Yes! However, a twinge of guilt pricked her. Knowing how straightforward Quaid was, she knew she could never consider his proposal without being just as honest.

"Quaid, I have to tell you something. The money . . . the trip. . . "

"I don't care where the money came from as long as you didn't rob a bank. I love you."

She threw her arms around his neck and kissed him on the cheek, tears running down her cheeks. "Yes, I'll marry you, Quaid Kincaid."

"You will? How soon?" He bolted upright.

"Before Summer comes," she said, rising, all aglow.

"Summer is a long way's off," he said frowning. "I was thinking of sometime sooner."

She took a hold of his hand and placed it on her belly. "Summer Kincaid will be here before you know it," she said beaming.

"Summer?" He said puzzled then grinned as he caught on. "Summer Kincaid. I like that, but maybe it should be Sumner."

"Next time," Page murmured, "next time."

THE END

ABOUT THE AUTHOR

C.J. CLARK currently lives in the Ozarks with her husband, ten cats and two dogs. Although a native Michigander, her heart is in Wyoming. She would love to hear from her readers.

E-mail her at writerbks@netscape.net or find her at www.cjclarkwrites.com and www.cjclarkauthor.webs.com

Printed in Great Britain
by Amazon.co.uk, Ltd.,
Marston Gate.